WITCH KARMA IN WESTERHAM

Paranormal Investigation Bureau Book 18

DIONNE LISTER

Copyright © 2022 by Dionne Lister

Imprint: Dionne Lister

Sydney, Australia

Contact: dionne@dionnelisterwriter.com

ISBN 9781922407207

Ebook edition

Cover art by Robert Baird

Editing by Hot Tree Editing

Proofreading L. Brodey

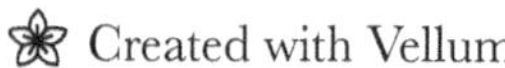 Created with Vellum

CHAPTER 1

Seven—the number of days since my loved ones and I had saved ourselves from an exploding house. Also the number of days I'd been in home detention because of the megaprice on my head, put there by a criminal organisation because I'd killed the leader's brother. Which meant it was also the number of days I'd had to train my squirrel army.

How much could you teach a squirrel in seven days? I was about to find out.

I stood on the grass in Angelica's backyard, about twenty feet from a squishy wrestling dummy that I'd dressed in T-shirt and shorts. My magic held it upright in the mid-morning sunshine. Ted lay at my feet, dozing. Abby, who'd made herself my 2IC, sat on the top of the timber picnic table and kept an eye on proceedings.

Before I turned around to look down at the squirrels, I smiled, then schooled my features to a businesslike façade—if I wanted the squirrels to take this seriously, I had to act the part. Once I had my face under control, I turned and surveyed the cuteness overload on the grass. I bit my top lip to keep from giggling. Why did they have to be so dang floofy? I cleared my throat. "Okay, so you all know the signal?" Thirty tiny heads nodded, and I bit my lip again. One little paw went up—a grey squirrel with a torn right ear. "Yes, Lefty?"

She chittered, which roughly translated in my mind to, *Two nuts, not one?*

"Yes. All the squirrels who get this right will get two nuts. If you get it wrong, no nuts." She nodded, and I surveyed all of them. "Any other questions before we start?" The smallest squirrel put up his hand. "Yes, Nano?"

A few little squeaks came out. *Nut now?*

"No. When you've done what we practised, you can have two nuts, but none now." I did my best to stay calm. If I showed frustration, they might balk and scatter. This was way harder than I assumed it would be. Although, I'd done pretty well to have them all standing together this still for as long as I had. I was sure I'd regret my next question, but I wanted to make sure they were okay with everything. "Any other questions?" A larger squirrel at the back, a grey with white tail, stood on her hind legs and waved her arm… or leg, or whatever. "Yes, Dusty." I hadn't told her that she was named after a feather duster, on account of her tail. Not that she'd probably care, but you never knew.

I love nuts.

Abby looked at me and rolled her eyes. Huh, I had no idea cats could do that. She shook her head. *Stupid squirrels. They're cute but not too bright. Cats are far superior.* She lifted her front paw to her mouth and licked.

I looked back at Dusty. "Yes, I know you do. All of you do. Right, no more questions. Wait for my signal." If I didn't just jump in and do this, we'd be here all night.

I turned back to face the dummy and held up my fist. I let my thumb unfurl for one, then my pointer finger for two, and when I released my middle finger, they took off in a bounding, leaping rush.

The back door opened, and Will, always sexy and dangerous-looking in his work suit, strode out. "Hey, Lily. What are you do—"

Nearly as one, my soldiers stopped and froze. Dusty was the first to break ranks and bolt for the nearest tree. That was all it took for the mass to bound and leap every which way for safety. Argh. Epic fail. My squirrel team had turned into a turmoil of squirrels—which really should be the collective noun for them. Maybe I should name my army Team Turmoil. I stared at Will, frustration pouring off me.

His eyebrows lifted. "What?" While trying not to smile, his gaze flicked to one remaining squirrel who, despite his comrades' freak out, had resumed his course. He'd climbed to the dummy's stomach and was biting the hell out of it.

"Argh. I was so close to success, and you ruined it with your ill-timed exit."

"It's good training for them, and better for you to deal with this now. Out in the field"—he snorted a quick laugh before pressing his lips together to stop it—"they're going to come up against surprises. If they freak out every time, they're going to be useless."

I hated that he was right. Why was there always more work to do?

The squirrel who'd succeeded didn't have a name yet. "You can stop biting now." He looked at me from his perch on the dummy's stomach and cocked his head to the side. "I think I'll call you Grey the Brave. Do you like that name?" He chittered, and a feeling of joy invaded my brain. They didn't always communicate in words or pictures; sometimes it was just emotion. I smiled. "Well, Grey the Brave, you get two nuts." His boofy tail twitched, and he leaped off the dummy and scampered to the table.

I moved to the picnic table with the little squirrel version on top, grabbed two nuts out of my pocket, and placed them there. A few of the deserter squirrels came down from their hiding places and slowly converged on the table. I shook my head. "Nope, sorry. You'll have to attack that dummy before you get your treats." I gave a nod at their target, then turned my gaze on Will. "Stay still, please."

He answered with a smirk.

Haphazardly, the squirrels rushed the dummy, reaching it a few at a time. Some ran up to the face and bit or scratched it, some attacked its back, some its arms, and some its legs. One enterprising squirrel even bit the dummy's bottom. I couldn't help giggling. Once they were all done, each presented to the tabletop, waiting patiently on their hind legs. Pride came through our bond loud and clear. Well, at least they'd done it eventually. It was a start.

I smiled. "Nuts for all. Good job!" I took some more nuts from the bags in my bulging shorts pockets and handed two to each squirrel. Once everyone was fed, I magicked the bags back to the kitchen cupboard.

"Are you finished now?"

"Yes. How was work?" Even though I was stuck at home, didn't mean anyone else was. Will, Angelica, and everyone else still had a job to do, so Will had started work at six this morning. We were pretty sure the directors knew we knew they were up to something, so Ma'am had given up the ruse that Chadiot was still in charge. It was only a matter of time till the directors cut the PIB off moneywise, and we were all in danger anyway, so four days ago, Ma'am told them that Chad had done a runner and she had no idea where he'd gone. Even if they figured we had him trapped, it didn't matter. Since then, they'd stayed quiet. The consensus was that they weren't ready to act yet, but they could be within days or weeks, so it was business as usual as far as crime-fighting was concerned. As far as surviving was concerned, Angelica was waiting for them to play their hand—she hinted she had a plan, but I wasn't so sure. Whatever happened, though, Chadiot was our insurance when it all went down. He was a witness to the directors' duplicity, and we needed him alive.

His amused expression fell. "We survived another morning, but I'll have to go back to work later. I thought I'd get away and have an early lunch with you."

"Why so busy?" Will had been working a couple of smaller assignments, but I didn't think Angelica had given him anything new to start on.

"I'm helping out with as many cases as I can—we all are." He made a bubble of silence. "Ma'am wants as many crimes solved and perpetrators arrested as possible. The timelines of a few missions have been moved up. A couple of instances of fraud, a recent drug bust in London, and a human trafficking case are all ones we were close to solving. She's almost given up on ones that we're not close to tying up. And since we don't know when we'll be cut off from our resources, she's decided to go this route."

I frowned and gave him a hug. "I suppose a few solved cases is better than leaving it all undone."

"Yes."

If only we could go back to the days where law enforcement was guaranteed. This whole thing was crazy. I cocked my head to the side. "Hmm, maybe Angelica could petition her contacts in parliament to fund a new agency. Then you could all quit—saving the directors from having you killed—and go straight to the new agency."

He gave me a sad smile. "Whilst that sounds good, the

whole idea is that the crims behind everything get a free pass to run their illegal operations. Whoever they can't buy off, they'll kill. We'd still be in danger."

"So we need to take them all out?" First Regula Pythonissam, now this. It really was never-ending. How had these criminal entities managed to put aside their differences to bribe the PIB? "How many groups are supporting the directors?"

"Two that we know of, maybe three. That's a lot of evil to disband and destroy. It could take us years and years, and that's doing it illegally. We can't just go around killing people, no matter how much better the world would be." His downcast expression made it obvious how disappointing he found that fact. For once, I had to agree that not being able to kill these evil crapheads was a bad thing.

"Surely the Queen and other leaders in this country won't want total chaos. That's what'll happen when they have free rein. That's another point in our favour to getting funding. Even if we'll all still be in danger, we'll have something positive. Maybe with the government's support and the directors out of the way, we can make a difference and stay alive."

Will's brow furrowed. "We can hope, Lily, but whatever happens, our path out of this is going to be the most dangerous thing the PIB agents have ever faced, and I have an inkling we'll need to be honest with the staff about what's going on. Which will be easier now that the directors know we know." He must've seen the distress on my face because he caressed my cheek. "Try not to worry. If there's a way out, I have no doubt that our team under Angelica's leadership can find it."

Abby had jumped down from her perch and did a figure eight around my legs, rubbing herself against me. *Don't worry. You are smart… for humans. You'll work it out.* Will must've heard, too, because we both chuckled.

I crouched down and picked her up. "Thanks for the vote of confidence." She nudged her head under my chin and purred.

Loud chittering came from the picnic table. We turned. All thirty of my students were on hind legs, tails twitching, as they stared at the sky. I tilted my head back and looked up.

A congealed mass of charcoal cloud blacked out the sun and blue sky. The roiling darkness got bigger, and flashes of lightning illuminated within it, setting off eerie green in the near blackness. Goosebumps cascaded along my arms, and I shivered.

That did not look good.

Will scooped up Ted and grabbed my arm. "Get inside. Now."

I wasn't going to ask questions, but before I ran inside, I made sure my friends were safe. I looked at my squirrel army. "Run! Get as far away as you can." I sent them a mental image of running away from a fox. I figured if they hadn't understood my words, they would understand that. "Go!" I waved my arms to scare them off. Grey the brave nodded—I swore it wasn't random—and he was off. The others followed in a streak of grey, up the large tree next to the back fence and over the other side to the reserve.

Will jerked my arm, and we sprinted inside. Being the last one in, I slammed the door, and not a moment too soon.

A sonic boom exploded outside. I jumped, and the windows rattled. Ted howled. A loud clunk reverberated through the kitchen as something hit the outside of the back wall. Ted, whining, scrambled out of Will's hold and slunk under the table. My eyes widened, and I jerked around, searching for any damage inside.

I sniffed. "It smells of magic." I blinked. I didn't know how it smelled of magic, and I'd never experienced it before, but I just knew. It was almost like the scent of ozone after a rain-storm, but sharper. A distinct wisp of acrid smoke stung my nose.

Lines indented Will's forehead. "We're under attack. The fact that you can smell it is something we'll talk about later. They must be nearby." He pulled out his phone. Right, so another unusual skill for me. At this point, I wasn't surprised. Not that smelling magic was helpful when the magic was already doing the damage. It was like not being able to smell a cowpat until you were stepping in it.

Thunder shook the house again, like literally shook it, and after a couple of seconds, a thud came from the back garden. I gripped the kitchen counter until the vibrations subsided.

Another explosion replete with blinding flash rocked the house. I dropped to the ground and pressed my back to the kitchen cupboards. Will, who stood with his legs wide and steady, looked down at me. "Make a shield, like you did at the house the other day."

"Okay." I'd expended a ridiculous amount of energy protecting myself and my loved ones from the leave-kill spell, but I'd recovered within a few days. The power I could wield without dying was increasing, and my recovery time was improving. So making a shield now was a cinch. I crawled under the table and placed a hand on Ted's back. "Abby, come here. I'll shield all of us." She calmly strutted to me and sat. Cats were so nonchalant. If only I could access some of her attitude.

"Good idea." Will gave a nod and sat on the floor, his aura bright with magic. "I'll call Angelica. I can't check the house-protection spells from here, and I don't want to go outside. Either she can come here, or we'll evacuate to your brother's."

You'd think we'd evacuate to the PIB, but without knowing what was going on, it was too risky. One of the compromised agents could be waiting for us. I just hoped James, Millicent, and my mum were okay. They were at HQ today. I was pretty sure Imani was out on assignment with Beren and Angelica. I crossed my fingers that they weren't in any danger. If they kept attacking us, Angelica and the others wouldn't be able to tidy up the last of their cases. *Argh, stop thinking. It's getting you nowhere.*

I took a deep breath, drew power, told the river what I wanted, and it materialised. A slight shimmer was the only evidence of the shield, like heat haze emanating from a bitumen road on a scorching summer day.

I wanted to ask Will how much longer he thought our protection spells would hold if they kept up the barrage, but he had the phone to his ear. And what would the neighbours think? My eyes widened. What if they went outside to look and got hurt? This was awful on so many levels.

"Hi, Ma'am. We have a problem." Will explained what was happening. Just as he stopped speaking to listen to Angelica, a sizzle echoed through the house. The deafening crack that followed had me slapping my hands to my ears. The force of the magic was like a punch to the gut, and I sucked in a breath.

Ted trembled. I ignored the throb in my stomach and placed a comforting hand on his back. "It's okay, boy. We're safe. I promise I won't let anything happen to you."

"Okay. Will do. Bye." Will crouched and looked at me. "We're out of here. Now. Bring Ted and Abby. I'll follow you."

"Shouldn't we go and look for those pigs, put an end to the attack? You said they should be close by."

"No. It's too dangerous. We have no idea where they are. They could be hiding in any of the houses in this street, and we'd be sitting ducks trying to find them." He must've seen the

I'm-about-to-argue look on my face because he scowled. "No, no, and no. We're leaving. Now!"

I blew out a breath. I wasn't crazy enough to think I could take them on by myself—there could be a full circle of them—and I wasn't about to put Will in danger because he had to run after me. "Okay." I picked Abby up and looked at Ted. "You heard him. We're going. I'll have to stand up over there." I nodded at the space near the kitchen door. "Come on." I crawled out from under the table, and Ted slunk out after me. Poor puppy. I stood and made sure my doorway wasn't going to take any pieces of furniture with me. I picked up Ted, just in case he wasn't sure how to go through a doorway safely. Then I made one and stepped through to my brother's reception room.

I'd been doing a fair bit of babysitting for James and Millicent lately, so they'd given me a key. I put the animals down and used the key to hurry in ahead of Will's arrival. As soon as we were safely in the vestibule, I called out, "Is anyone home? It's Lily."

Millicent's answering shout reached me at the same time Will came through his doorway. "I'm just in the kitchen feeding Annabelle. Come in."

I headed for the kitchen, my tribe following. Millicent had Annabelle in a high chair and was feeding her some kind of orange goop. Mill smiled. "What are you guys doing here?" She glanced up at the wall clock. "Shouldn't you be home having lunch?"

"Didn't Angelica call you?"

Will looked at me. "She probably hasn't had time. She was contacting James first and checking on HQ." He looked at Mill. "Angelica's house is under attack from a cloud concoction."

Two divots appeared between her brows. "What?"

"A dark billowing cloud came out of nowhere. Lily's squirrels noticed it first." He glanced at me, an unreadable look on his face. His gaze moved back to Millicent. "They hit the house several times. I'm thinking they made their magic look like lightning bolts, so anyone seeing it had some rational way to explain it. From what we could tell, there's damage to the outside of the house, but we couldn't check. They were still firing at us when we left."

I scratched the back of my neck. "I don't know if the house will even be standing by the time we return." I bit my lip. "Can they tell we've left?"

"No," said Will. He closed his mouth, and his jaw muscles bunched. If I could guess, I'd say he was rather angry.

Annabelle waved her hands around. "Ga, ga, mmmm, mmmm."

"Sorry, sweetie. Mummy's a bit distracted." She slid another spoonful of food into Annabelle's mouth, and my adorable niece kicked her legs in happiness. After Millicent gave Annabelle another spoonful, she said, "If the house is destroyed, you can stay here."

I shook my head vehemently. "No way. They want me most of all, and I won't bring that danger to your doorstep. We can stay in a hotel. If we travel there, they'll have no idea where we are." Since living at Angelica's, Will had rented out his place, and even if he hadn't, that was probably an obvious place to go, so there was no sense in going there.

Will's phone rang. "Hello, Ma'am." He nodded as he listened. "Okay. Yes." He put one hand on his hip. "Right. Bye." He hung up and slid his phone into his pocket. "She wants us to meet her at her country place… take the danger away from here." He looked at Millicent. "James is coming home shortly, and your dad's coming over. They're going to upgrade your protections."

"What about Angelica's house?" Millicent wiped food off Annabelle's face with the baby's bib.

Will's poker expression settled in place. "They'll check on it later. Whatever will be, will be."

I frowned, and Millicent met my sad gaze. "It'll be okay, Lily. They won't have levelled it, and any damage can be fixed. The most important things are safe." She glanced at Ted and Abby, then up at me and Will and smiled. "You know I'm right."

I sighed. "Yeah, yeah, I know. Still… that's home. Argh, and you know who's still at the country house?"

Millicent chuckled. "Our favourite person."

"Yes." I'd managed to avoid having to see Chadiot since everything had gone down a week ago. If I never saw him again, I wouldn't shed a tear. Looked like I might just have to have a little cry later.

Will laughed. "It's a big house. We'll make sure to avoid the lounge room."

Annabelle made gah, gah, gah noises and slammed her tiny hands on her high chair tray a few times. Millicent laughed. "Okay, missy, let's free you from your confines, and you can have a play." Ah, to be a baby again and have nothing to worry about. Although, did I want to suffer through every-thing again—losing my parents, James going missing, finding out witches existed, and the search and battle for my mother? Hmm, maybe not.

"Here, let me get her out. I want to give her a cuddle before we leave. I may not be back here for a while." Millicent had already unclipped Annabelle's seat belt thing, and I slid my hands under her armpits and lifted her out. She cooed at me, and I smiled. "You are the cutest thing ever." I blew a raspberry on her chubby cheek, and she giggled.

Millicent cocked her head to the side, and she got a *look*. "You're so good with her."

"Ha, no way! I'm not close to being ready for one of these, no matter how cute they are or how much I love Annabelle. I can give her back when I've had enough." I laughed.

Will wore a thoughtful expression. "But you do want them… one day."

I shrugged. "Yes and no. I'd be so scared something would happen to them, and after what I went through with Mum and Dad…. Well…." I didn't want to finish that because what if Millicent thought I was judging her and James. I blew another raspberry on my niece's cheek. "She's enough for now. Why don't we talk about this when there's no price on my head? Now's not the ideal time to be thinking about the future."

Millicent's shoulders sagged. "You're right. Sorry. I forget sometimes when I'm here in my safe cocoon. But we'll all get through this. There's no bunch of more capable witches. We all have your back, Lily, and there's no way Angelica will let the PIB go without the fight of her life."

I sighed and gave my niece a kiss on the cheek. "I'll see you soon, sweetie. Be good for Mummy." I handed her to Millicent, and gave Millicent a kiss on the cheek too.

"James and I will come and visit. We won't let you get too bored."

Will's phone rang. He looked at the caller details, then at me. "Time to go. Angelica's waiting." He answered the phone. "We're coming right now." He hung up and made a doorway. I made mine, and with a wave to Mill and Annabelle, and sadness at having to run from a home I'd come to love, I stepped through. I hoped that one day my life would be simple and safe and *normal*. The alternative didn't bear thinking about.

CHAPTER 2

When we arrived at the country house, Angelica answered the reception-room door. Immaculately dressed in her black-and-white uniform, her hair in a tidy bun, poker face in situ, she was the epitome of a strong, calm leader who was in total control. The lie of being in total control was one I appreciated she made, and the fact she could convey calmness in the face of her whole world falling apart, well, we were lucky she was the one calling the shots.

I went inside first, Ted and Abby at my heels, and stood to the side. *Please don't suggest going to the living room.* Angelica eyed the animals. "Oh, good idea bringing them. We might not return for a while." There was no point asking how long a while was. She didn't have a crystal ball.

Will came in and shut the door. "What's happening at HQ?"

Angelica made a bubble of total silence. "Nothing unusual. I have your mother and Olivia working in my office under special protection spells. No one can get in unless I give permission, and if Kat or Olivia say a certain safe word, my phone will buzz, and I'll go straight there. They can come and go as they please, of course. James is keeping an eye on the agents we know are working for the directors. It's not ideal, but we can't afford not to." She took in a loud breath through her nose and pushed it out again. "If only there were more agents we could trust."

"Thank you for not using my sister. She and Lavender aren't ready to face this threat yet." It was true they were new to the agenting thing, but both were strong witches in their own right. Will's anxiety for his sister was the main reason Angelica kept them out of it as much as she could. Will was already distracted, having me to worry about—he didn't need that extra stress.

"Yes, well, we might need to revisit that decision, but not today." She ignored Will's raised brow and looked past me to the living room. "Why don't we convene in my study. I don't much fancy standing here for our meeting." Without waiting for an answer, she strode down the hallway, all the way to an open door at the end.

I looked at Will and shrugged in a "what can you do" way, then followed Angelica. Will's unimpressed stare told me exactly what he thought about giving in and letting his sister help. Unluckily for him, when it came down to it, he had no say.

Angelica's study was nothing like I expected and the opposite of her office at the PIB. A faded cream-coloured Persian rug covered most of the polished timber floor. The eggshell-blue walls were calming, and the view of her garden through multi-paned windows was stunning. She sat on an armchair behind her desk—an unusual choice for an office chair. The pattern on it mirrored that of the two armchairs that she gestured Will and I to sit in—fawn background with teal, red, blue, and yellow butterflies. "This fabric is gorgeous."

She didn't smile, but her tone was friendly. "Thank you, dear. I had the chairs specially made. Now, as much as I'd love to discuss my décor, I'm afraid we have more pressing things to talk about." She directed her gaze at Will. "What happened?"

Will explained everything from the time the squirrels alerted us to our escape to Millicent's. "The safest would be to deploy a drone to check out the damage."

"No need. James is sending one of our compromised agents there. If we have to risk someone, it might as well be them." Her sharklike smile had returned, and I grinned—there was no faulting her thinking. She folded her hands together on her desk. "James has also intercepted police radio discussion about the attack that was called in by worried neighbours. As far as they're concerned, a freak storm gathered, and the house was struck by multiple lightning bolts. It's cleared now."

I folded my arms. "So, what are we supposed to do? We can't exactly go after them yet. Even if we assumed which crime family attacked us, it's foolish to retaliate at this stage."

Her satisfied smile surprised me. "Good summation, dear." Her poker face displaced her smile. "As much as it galls me, we'll wait for our chance. I have things I need to put in place before we destroy them."

"How long are we staying here?" asked Will.

"I'm not sure. At least a week, maybe longer." Argh, why? Angelica scrutinised me. "What is the sneer for? Isn't this place grand enough for you?"

"Of course it is—it's beautiful. But being this close to Chad without torturing him just a little bit will be… challenging."

Will turned to me. "What kind of torture are you thinking?"

"Hmm, a bit of electrocution, maybe disappearing his eyebrows, and my old favourite, making him feel like he's wet himself." I chuckled at the memory of the cab driver.

Angelica gave me a stern look. "Are you ever going to grow up, dear?"

I pretended to think about it. After a while, I shook my head. "Nope. Growing up is overrated."

She gave me a look and opened her mouth, but before she could tell me how inadequate she found that, her phone rang. She took it out of her jacket pocket and held it to her ear. "Hello, Agent DuPree speaking." Angelica listened for a couple of minutes. Had her eyebrows risen a fraction of a millimetre? Hmm. I hated that I couldn't read poker faces. The PIB agents had them down to a fine art. If I was honest, I'd admit that I was sad I didn't have their skills. My face gave away my thoughts and feelings louder than a sign in all caps with someone articulating it through a loudspeaker simultaneously. "I'll be there shortly with two of my agents. Okay. Goodbye." Angelica stood and looked at Will. "We have a new case to attend immediately."

Will stood. "I thought we weren't taking on anything new. We don't have time."

She smoothed her jacket lapel. "For this person, we do."

"Ooh, who is it?" I couldn't stand not knowing things. Not that I thought she'd tell me, but it was worth a shot.

"Phillip Humphries. He's served in our parliament, and he's one of the richest men in England. His first cousin's daughter has just been murdered. He's very close with his first cousin, and he's asked us to handle this. It occurred at a witch-owned company, so they called the PIB straight away. As per my instructions, James told them we couldn't attend. Phillip never takes no for an answer." She pressed her lips together, then shook her head. I wasn't sure if she had an issue with privileged people demanding things, or she was feeling the pressure of having such a high-profile person to please. Solving this crime would mean one or even two others wouldn't get finalised. Why was this family so important? Was it just because they were rich?

"Doesn't he donate heavily to help impoverished non-witches?"

"Yes, William, he does. I also… owe him a favour, so I can't say no." As much as I wanted to know this bit of information, it was none of my business, so I kept my mouth closed. If Angelica knew how I'd controlled myself, she would've been proud.

I stood. "Right, well, before you go, can you tell me which is Will's and my room? I might as well make myself comfortable."

"No, dear. You're coming with us."

Will and I both said, "What?" at the same time.

"But you said you were taking two agents." I was sure that's what she'd said.

"Yes, I did. You're one of them—I could hardly say I'm taking one agent and Lily." She shook her head is if to say, "why do I have to answer such silly questions." "You can take photos, if necessary. I don't know how she died, and no one will know what you're doing. I want to be as efficient as possible on this one. We have limited time, as you well know."

Will looked at me. "Best get your uniform on, and let's get going."

I wasn't sure how far away this country house was from home, but I was pretty sure my magic was strong enough to move my uniform from there to here. "Okay." I drew a chunk of magic from the river. "Dress me in my uniform and simultaneously put the clothes I'm wearing, except for my underwear, on that chair." I looked at the chair I'd just vacated.

As my clothes appeared on the chair, Will chuckled. "I remember that time you forgot to exclude your underwear." He waggled his brows.

I rolled my eyes. "Yes, and you're never going to let me live it down, are you?"

"Nope."

Angelica kept her poker face intact, but I could see the mirth shining in her eyes. "I'll make the doorway, and we can all use it." Just as we stepped through, I realised Abby and Ted hadn't followed us into the study. They were probably checking out their new home. Which reminded me—I'd have to magic Abby's litter tray into the laundry. Hopefully she could hold on until we returned.

We exited into a swanky black-marble-floored reception room furnished with a white leather couch, a side table with a glass vase containing red and black tulips, and what looked like original oil paintings on the walls. The heavy expense of it swirled in my nostrils. How was it that richness had an odour? My nose was really getting a workout today.

The whole front wall leading to the main reception area was glass. That was new—a reception room where people could see you arriving. They obviously didn't get non-witches in, or maybe only ones who already knew about witches. A golden plaque running across the top of the exit doors proclaimed Fairchild Finance.

Angelica buzzed the intercom. "Agent DuPree from the Paranormal Investigation Bureau."

The door chimed and automatically opened outward. I

looked at the door with my other sight, and there was a spell I couldn't decipher—probably the automatic-opening thing, or maybe it was a security spell, and the door was electronically operated. I'd never know.

"Lily, are you coming?" Will stared at me from outside while Angelica approached the reception desk.

"Oh, sorry." It would be nice to be able to keep focus just once in my life. At least I could do it when it counted. That's what mattered. I stepped out of the reception room, and the door automatically shut.

The black marble underfoot continued in the foyer, making the jet-black reception desk look like a monolith growing from the floor. The gorgeous blonde twenty-something behind the desk nodded at whatever Angelica had said. She stood, and her eyes found Will. Who knew someone could switch from professional to sultry-looking in less than half a second? Angelica followed the woman's gaze and turned to see Will. She didn't roll her eyes, but her expression said she was dying to. *You and me both, Ma'am.*

Having a hot fiancé wasn't all it was cracked up to be sometimes. When equally hot women looked at him like that, I couldn't do anything but question how long it would be until he strayed. Not that he'd ever made me feel that way, but being a realist, there was a chance that one of these women would get her way eventually.

Angelica turned back to the almost-salivating woman. "Can you show us to the body, please?"

Her gaze slowly made its way to Angelica. "Of course. Come this way." She smiled at Will before turning and leading us through a large timber door to the right of her desk.

Will grabbed my hand. I blinked. He was doing this at work—he never showed affection on the job, which was only sensible. Shame heated my cheeks. I needed to stop worrying. He leaned down and whispered in my ear, "I love you. No one else compares. I never want you to doubt how much I love you, my Aussie witch."

"I know. I'm sorry." I gave him an apologetic smile. "I guess we'd better hurry up."

Angelica had disappeared through the door. Will released my hand, and we got a move on.

The hallway beyond the door carved a path between glass-fronted offices. Some were see-through, and others were greyed out. Was that a feature of the glass that could be turned on and off? I'd seen something about that on a TV show once—it was done with electricity rather than magic, although that seemed pretty magical to me. Even electricity was a wonder, and how did information fly across the air and turn into a picture on a TV screen or music on the radio? How much of the technology humans had came from witches? Or did humans have a kind of magic themselves?

At the end of the aisle, it dog-legged right and kept going, but we stopped at an open door to a greyed-out room. The receptionist stood in the doorway, speaking to a middle-aged man in a suit. His thick brown hair was slicked back in a style I would call sleaze. I was so judgemental sometimes, but I didn't think I'd met a man with that hairstyle who wasn't trying to sell me something dodgy. To be fair to the man, his shoulders drooped, and shock emanated from his face. He looked stupefied.

The receptionist stood back and introduced Agent DuPree from the Paranormal Investigation Bureau to a red-eyed Mr Fairchild. I assumed the redness was from crying, not because he was a vampire or something. They shook hands while the receptionist made come-hither eyes at Will, who frowned and turned to shake Mr Fairchild's hand. Will turned to me. "And this is Agent Bianchi, our invaluable forensics photographer." *What the…?*

Mr Marcus Fairchild held out his hand to me. I recovered from my surprise and shook his hand. "Good to meet you." I didn't want to say lovely because we weren't exactly at a cocktail party.

"Come in, please. My—my wife is over here." He gritted his teeth, maybe to stop further tears.

As soon I crossed the threshold into what appeared to be a conference room, the sickly-sweet stench I knew only too well had me putting my hand over my nose. I wasn't the only one. Will magicked a hanky to himself and placed it over his nose. Ma'am had magicked on a white mask that made her look like she was about to sand something with a power tool.

We reached the body. Mrs Fairchild lay face up on the ground, her blonde hair melted into what looked like a hard cap on her head. I wasn't about to touch it to find out. Her forehead was blackened and blistered. The part of her silk shirt resting atop her heart was also burnt, some of it missing to expose the singed skin underneath. Ouch.

A woman in her thirties and a man who looked to be in his fifties stood next to the body. The woman, in a red designer-looking suit, had her arms folded. A scowl twisted her face. Was she angry that Mrs Fairchild had died, or had someone accused her? The man tapped his shoe on the ground and gazed around the space, as if he was bored waiting for a train.

Angelica turned a stern face towards them. "I understand you were the only people with her when she died?" They nodded. "What happened?"

The woman's mouth remained closed, and her chin raised in a defiant gesture. The man rubbed his hand on the back of his neck and met Angelica's gaze. "We were finishing our meeting, sitting just there"—he pointed to the two chairs that weren't pushed in under the table—"when lightning came out of nowhere and hit her. It struck her head and another bit snaked out and hit her chest."

Angelica looked up. There was nothing to see except ceiling and downlights. "And you were the only three in here?"

He nodded. Angelica turned to Will. "Get Agent Bianchi *senior* here and Agent Floyd from forensics." She obviously had questions about why I'd suddenly been promoted. *You and me both, Ma'am.* Although, technically, she'd started it by saying she'd bring two agents.

"Yes, Ma'am." Will pulled his phone out and went into the hall.

Angelica turned to the two workers. "Please go to your offices. I'll have someone here to interview you shortly."

The man nodded, but the woman shook her head. "I'm not speaking to anyone without a solicitor present." Mr Fairchild's brow furrowed, and he stared at her. She stared back. I had no idea what was going on. Maybe he suspected her, and she wasn't amused? If she was a loyal employee and innocent, I didn't blame her for being upset. Not to mention she'd just seen someone murdered up close.

Angelica looked at Mr Fairchild. "I'd like you to wait in your office as well."

He sighed. "I know the husband is usually the number-one suspect, but I wasn't even in the room. I loved my wife." He glanced at the body, then whipped his gaze back to Angelica. It looked as if it pained him to see her body, but was it heartbreak or guilt?

"Yes, husbands are always considered in these cases. I wouldn't be doing my job properly if my agents didn't interview you. Do you want us to get to the bottom of what happened to your wife?" If I didn't know better, I'd think Ma'am had already begun her interrogations.

His eyes widened. "Of course I want you to get to the bottom of it." He looked at his employees. "Get to your offices. If you want a solicitor, Jasmin, call one now." Mr Fairchild watched his employees leave—maybe wondering which one killed his wife—and then followed them out.

Angelica turned to me and made a bubble of silence. "Can you please take normal photos and then your special ones?"

"Can do."

She crouched next to the body and looked up at me. "Make sure you photograph the whole room. You never know where a clue will turn up."

"Yes, Ma'am." I figured since I was an honorary agent, I should behave like one, which meant addressing her by her professional title. Angelica disappeared her spell.

Will stuck his head in the door. "Do you need me, Ma'am, or would you prefer that I join James for the interviews?"

She answered without taking her eyes off the body. "Go with Agent Bianchi. You two make a good interview team."

"Yes, Ma'am." Will gave me a smile and went back into the hall.

I drew power from the river and magicked my camera to myself. Thank goodness it had survived the attack. Since it was in okay condition, we could assume the house was still standing; plus, no authorities had contacted Angelica to tell her that her house had been destroyed. Hopefully the picnic table bore the brunt of the attack, being out of the house's protective bubble. As long as my squirrels were safe, I was fine. A house could be fixed.

Argh, why was that smell so bad? Hmm. I drew more magic. "Create an invisible bubble around my head that is sealed to the outside so I can't smell that stench." I pictured one of those huge ancient diving helmets for the size. The sense of space closing in around my head and face tipped me off that it had worked. I sniffed, then smiled. No stinky burned person. Yay, me.

Angelica eyed me. "Did you just enclose your head in an invisible shield?"

"Yep." I couldn't help sounding proud. Maybe I'd just invented a way all agents could save their olfactory senses when dealing with dead bodies.

"You might want to be careful, dear. After a few minutes, you'll use up your oxygen. Please get rid of it before you faint or die." She turned back to the body and resumed her perusal.

Oh. Trust her to go and ruin my fun and prove that I wasn't nearly as smart as I thought. Every. Freaking. Time. I sighed and disappeared the bubble. Next time I'd come prepared with a hanky soaked in lavender or citrus oil.

I tried to ignore the smell, and my ineptitude, and moved around the room, taking photos of everything from every angle, including the body. Mrs Fairchild was dressed in a cream-silk blouse and an expensive-looking pink skirt and jacket. Her nails had been freshly done in a matching blush colour. What looked like diamond studs sparkled from her ears, and three diamond rings graced her fingers, and that didn't include the rock on her wedding finger. "How old was she?"

"Forty-four," Angelica answered.

"She looks about thirty. Kept in shape, no wrinkles. She must use Botox and fillers." Her lips were certainly larger than normal. At least they were covered in lipstick, and we couldn't see the blue of death. It was a small win, but I'd take it. This scene was grizzly enough.

I photographed her expensive gold-and-diamond-encrusted Cartier watch. I checked my phone for the time.

Yep, the watch had stopped when she'd been zapped. A crack zigzagged across the glass. I shuddered. After numerous times almost being struck by magic lightning and being a zapper myself, I dreaded thinking of what that must've felt like. At least it would've been quick.

"Do you think one of those two did it?" I asked.

"That would be my first thought." Angelica looked at the ceiling. "If someone was in the room above, the fatal shock would've come from there, and there'd be a hole in the ceiling."

I checked the ceiling with my other sight. "There's no evidence of magic, so they haven't fixed it in the last day or two."

"Exactly."

"Hello." James walked through the door, and his face scrunched up. "Ew, that's ripe."

Angelica gave him a deadpan look. "Tell me something I don't know. You're excused to go and interview the two employees who were in the room with her."

"Will told me. I thought I'd stop in here on the way and let you know I'd arrived. Meeting at HQ when this is over?"

She cocked her head to the side. "No. The place Lily and Will are staying."

"Ah, okay. I'll message you when I'm done here. You want me to interview the husband and the deceased's assistant too?"

"Yes, please. The woman who was here when it happened has solicitored up. If you can't speak to her today, please do it ASAP tomorrow."

"Okay. Will do. Anything else?"

She shook her head. "No. See you later, Agent Bianchi."

James turned and left, and another man entered. He looked to be in his forties, about six foot even, with curly blond hair that was, unlike most other agents, gathered in a short ponytail at the back of his head. His lithe build and easy movements were that of a man half his age. "Agent Floyd reporting for duty, Ma'am. What have we got here?"

I stepped out of the way, and Ma'am moved over to give him access to the body. The victim was lying next to a wall, so we couldn't all stand around her as if she were a table or bonfire. A smile threatened. Oh my God! What was wrong with me? *That wasn't funny, brain. Have some respect.*

I took a deep breath. Time to use my talent. I eyed Agent Floyd. He wasn't on the list of compromised agents, and if Angelica trusted him to be here while I did my thing, I'd have to trust him too. It's not like he'd know why I was working with magic drawn; besides, all his focus was on the body. I opened to the river of power. *Show me who killed Mrs Fairchild.*

My viewfinder was a portal to darkness. I closed my eyes and opened them again. Still black. I took a photo anyway, just so I could show Angelica. Maybe she could figure out what it meant? It certainly wasn't black in here when she was struck. Did it mean the person had been somewhere else when they cast the spell? If so, why was there no evidence of it? Had someone been standing outside, and Jasmin and her colleague couldn't see them because the glass was greyed out?

I stepped into the corridor. *Show me who killed Mrs Fairchild.* I turned three hundred and sixty degrees. Inky murk obscured my view. I lowered my Nikon. It didn't make sense. It couldn't have been pitch-black here this morning. Or was my magic trying to tell me it couldn't figure it out? I supposed nothing in life was perfect, and magic must have its limits. I sighed loudly. Of all the times for my talent to fail, it had to be the one where Angelica was trying to help one of her most powerful acquaintances. Hopefully, James would have more luck.

Figuring Angelica was going to be a while, and not wanting to return to the country house alone, I wandered along the corridor. I passed a greyed-out office with an ajar door. Someone whispered something I couldn't hear, and people laughed. It could be two or three voices, but it was hard to tell with just laughter. Why were they happy the morning one of their bosses was killed? Surely they didn't want to upset Mr Fairchild. Imagine if he caught them being jovial. If only they weren't witches and could tell if someone cast a spell, I'd listen in with magic. The best I could do was pretend to take photos and loiter outside hoping they'd say something loud enough for me to decipher.

The hushed voice of a woman said, "Ding dong, the wicked old witch is dead."

"Karma, baby. Karma," said a man. Then they laughed again.

Not wanting to push my luck, I returned to the office. Angelica was standing, watching Agent Floyd. She turned her head towards me. "How did you go?"

I shook my head. "I've gotten all the *normal* photos."

One eyebrow crept up her forehead. "Okay, dear." She approached me. "Why don't you let me have a look?" I brought up the last photo on the screen and handed the camera over so she could scroll through. She finished looking at them and handed it back. "Yes, very normal." She tapped her chin. "Hmm." Turning to Agent Floyd, she said, "I have something to do. When you're finished, call me, but don't go back to headquarters. Meet me at the Cauldron and Broom." I couldn't help grinning. So not subtle. I assumed it was a pub for witches or at least a pub named by someone who liked the whole witch vibe.

"Yes, Ma'am. Will do."

"Come with me." Angelica strode past me and out the door. I followed her back to the reception area. She spoke to Will's fangirl. "Excuse me."

She smiled. "Yes. How can I help?"

"Who owns the office above the conference room?"

"We do, but they're undergoing refurbishment… well, they will be as of next week. We moved out of there two months ago."

"I need to go up there and have a look. Is that possible right now?"

"Yes, of course. Just a moment." She opened one of her drawers and took out a tag. Her magic came to life—confident with a hint of devil-may-care. Interesting. What a weird one to have. Maybe it meant she enjoyed living dangerously, or maybe it had to do with having a desire to cause trouble? She handed the tag to Angelica. "You're all set. It's temporary and will give you access via the lift for twenty-four hours."

Angelica took the tag. "Thank you. We'll be back shortly."

We walked to the bank of three lifts that sat to the right of the reception room. Angelica pressed the Up button. While we waited, Mr Fairchild came through the door from the office section. He looked at Angelica. "Where are you going?" His timing was interesting. Had he been watching us on security camera, or did he have a listening spell or something at reception? Maybe it was as simple as Will's fangirl letting him know what was going on.

Angelica replied calmly and with authority steeling her words. "I need to investigate further. I would appreciate it if you returned to your office until your interview is concluded."

He stared at her, and the lift arrived with a ding. He jumped. Nervous much? "I've changed my mind. I want my solicitor involved."

"Of course you do," Angelica replied as the lift doors opened. "Call them now and have them attend ASAP."

His lips pressed together, and his gaze darkened. The CEO of a successful company, he probably wasn't used to being ordered around. "I know you'll try and pin this on me, but I loved my wife. I didn't kill her. I wasn't even in the room with her when she died, for goodness' sake."

Angelica simply nodded slowly, her expression that of a parent not believing a child. "We don't try and pin anything on anyone. The evidence tells us who did it. If you have nothing to hide, then you have nothing to worry about." She stuck her hand in between the closing lift doors so that they opened again, and she stepped inside. Angelica missed seeing Mr Fairchild's pressed-together lips and tightened fists, but I didn't.

The lift doors closed. Angelica swiped her card and pressed Level 16. I made a bubble of total silence. "He didn't look overly happy when you got in the lift."

"I'm sure he didn't, dear." It was a short trip to the next floor, and Angelica didn't elaborate. Did she think he'd done it, or was she just keeping all the options open until we'd dug further?

The lift doors opened to a darkened hallway. Angelica's magic tickled my scalp, and a ball of light hovered over her upturned palm. The floors had been stripped back to concrete, and sections of framing were gone, leaving a large open area beyond where the reception desk was situated on the floor below. Some of the strip fluorescent lighting panels were missing, and white electrical wires hung down from a couple of them. *Hmm, that's not safe.* From the looks of the remaining ceiling panels and handful of office cubicles, this area had last been renovated twenty years ago. Maybe that's when the building had been constructed? I had no idea, though, as I hadn't seen the outside.

We headed for the area at the back of this level that would correspond to the conference room, careful to avoid any dangling wires. We stopped at a door in a smooth timber-panelled wall. There was another door next to it—maybe two offices? Just as Angelica was about to open one of the doors, her phone rang.

"Yes, Agent Bianchi?" Angelica's brow furrowed, and her light extinguished. "I'll send you the coordinates right now. Stand by." My heart rate kicked up a notch. Angelica's voice had an edge to it, one she rarely displayed. "Did you get it?" The silence as Angelica waited for the answer was heavier than the impenetrable blackness around us. I held my breath, waiting. "Good. Now go! Call me when you get there."

I made a ball of light. It reflected off a concerned Angelica. *Not good.* "What happened?"

"Hold on a moment, dear." She must be worried if she'd stopped everything to wait for the call. After a few uncomfortable moments, her phone rang. "Angelica here." Her shoulders relaxed, and she nodded. "Good. Okay. I'll tell James. We'll be back in about an hour…. Yes, take any bedroom you like, except for mine, of course. Bye." She looked at me and made a bubble of silence. "They attacked your brother's house, but everyone's safe, including the dogs and rats. Millicent's taken everyone to the country house."

A weighty wet blanket of guilt slopped over me. Why didn't I have self-control? I shouldn't have killed that man. Why hadn't I figured out how to disable people rather than kill them yet? I found myself in dangerous situations time and again, and my first instinct was to strike a murderous blow first and never even ask questions. Things needed to change. I wasn't only jeopardising my life, but those of the people I loved. I'd figure out something while we spent time at Angelica's country place.

Angelica stared at me. "It's not your fault, Lily. This has been coming for a long time."

I checked my mind shield was up. Yep. Must be my shouty facial expression. "But if I hadn't killed the crime boss's br—"

Angelica put up her hand. "His brother was an evil waste of space. You did the world a favour. Besides, they'd eventually have come for us anyway, with the blessing and encouragement of the directors. Now, enough of this…." She waved her hand around. "We have work to do." She magicked a pair of rubber gloves on and opened the door to one of the offices and went inside. If my estimations were correct, we were going to be standing directly over Mrs Fairchild's body.

Before I got too far into the room, Angelica looked at me. "Can you do your thing, dear? I'll look for magic signatures and evidence of spells."

"Yes, Ma'am." I drew magic and turned my camera on, then lifted it to my face. *Show me the person who killed Mrs Fairchild.* The room didn't change, not even to black everything out. Hmm. "Nothing. Room looks the same as before."

She stared at me but gave nothing away. "Wait here until I'm finished; then we'll go to the office next door."

"Okay." While she worked, I wandered the empty room. There was nothing to see in the windowless space but blank walls. So uninspiring. Hmm. I lifted my camera again. *Show me Mrs Fairchild last time she was in this room.*

The light brightened and took on an unhealthy, fluorescent tinge. A middle-aged woman dressed in a pale-blue shirt looked across the table at Mrs Fairchild. The woman's pinched face was a mixture of frustration and anger. Mrs Fairchild pointed a ruby-red, sharp talon at her. I clicked a picture, walked to the other side to face Mrs Fairchild, and took a different picture. A desktop computer was on. The date on the screen was March eighteenth this year.

Show me the employee's name. The scene changed. Mrs Fairchild was gone, and the lady in the blue shirt now wore a black cashmere jumper. She was looking at an email on her desktop screen. Her email sign off was Marian Arthur, Head of Accounting. I took another picture. This was a dingy, small office for someone with her responsibilities at such a large, prestigious firm.

Had she had anything to do with it, or was it just a coincidence that her old office happened to be on top of the scene of the crime? Most of the time, my magic showed me relevant stuff, but I had asked a specific question, and my magic had complied. Maybe what I'd just seen was random? Nevertheless, I'd show Angelica.

To test whether it really meant much, I'd have to conduct more research. "Can I go into another area of this place? I need to take more photos."

She turned to look at me. "Okay. If you go into the room next door, wear gloves to open it. And be careful not to trip on anything. Make a light."

My eye twitched as I bit back a retort that went something along the lines of, for goodness' sake, as if I was going to stumble around in the dark and not make a light. I also commended myself on not rolling my eyes. "Of course." I stopped just outside the door and made a bobbing light, but I set it to hover just in front of my stomach. That way, it wouldn't blind me or make it hard to take a photo. Instead of going next door—I didn't want to accidentally ruin any evidence—I made my way to the left, along what would be the downstairs hallway.

Hmm. I halted and drew magic, then looked through my camera. "Show me the office layout from three months ago." Light bloomed, and an intact office appeared. It was different from downstairs, so I was careful to lower the camera when I started walking. Every now and then, I checked where I was walking in real time because randomly, small mounds of debris

—a chair, pile of papers, or unattached door—were occupying space on the floor, and I didn't want to trip over them.

There weren't plaques on every office door through my camera, but it seemed the heads of departments had them. I stopped in front of a door that read Allan Heard, Operations Manager. I lowered my camera and stepped across the threshold of what used to be his office. It was now just a concrete-floored space with half the ceiling panels missing and no walls. I stood at the "doorway" and lifted my camera to my face. "Show me the last time Mrs Fairchild was in this office."

My mouth dropped open. I clicked off a shot. She was sitting in his office chair, alone, and going through one of his top drawers. What an invasion of privacy. What had he done to attract that kind of attention from her?

I moved close to where she sat and focussed the camera on the drawer she was rummaging in. I took a shot to examine later. I couldn't really see anything of import, but it was likely I didn't know what constituted important business information and what didn't.

Onto the next office.

This time I picked Annie Jones, Head of HR. I lifted my camera once again. "Show me the last time Mrs Fairchild was in here." The deceased woman stood on the same side of the desk as Ms Jones sat. A laptop was open in front of them. Mrs Fairchild wore what I would class as a sarcastic smile. Annie scowled as Mrs Fairchild pointed to something on the screen. I went around and took a photo of it. It was a report of some kind. I clicked off a photo, then lowered my camera to again be surrounded by a dark, desolate space. At least my bobbing light ball was still there.

Angelica appeared out of the gloom. "There you are, dear. Are you having any luck?"

"I haven't taken anything to do with the killer. At least, I don't think so, but I have got something. I just don't know what it is."

She gave me a curious look. "You took photos?"

"Yes."

"Good. Do you need to take any more?"

It wouldn't hurt, but if it was all just going to be photos of Mrs Fairchild annoying people, what was the point? She was a boss. It's what they did. It didn't mean any of those workers had a reason to kill her. "No. I don't know how relevant my pictures are. It could just be my magic trying to show me something rather than nothing, even if it's not crucial."

She gave a nod. "Right. We'll get going and look at them at the pub."

"Okay." My stomach grumbled loudly, but I was beyond being embarrassed. Angelica knew my weirdnesses by now.

Angelica smirked. "Yes, dear, you can get something to eat while we're there."

I smiled. "Ha, thanks." We were being careful about where we went, but by going via doorway, there was little chance the bad guys would have any idea where I was. Maybe it was safer to jump from spot to spot rather than staying somewhere they knew I lived?

We made our way back to the lift. At the next floor down, the door opened, and we stepped out. The receptionist was giving Will come-hither eyes. Grrr. His voice reached us. "Can you tell me where my fiancée is?"

She gave him a puzzled look. "Who?"

"The agent I came here with, the young, gorgeous one with the blue eyes."

I grinned. Aw, he was such a sweetie. "Hey."

The receptionist frowned at me, and Will turned and smiled. "Hey. Where did you disappear to?"

Angelica answered, "We wanted to have a look upstairs. What about you and Agent Bianchi Senior?"

"We have a few more interviews to conduct, but the remaining people have asked a solicitor be present. We'll get them to come to HQ tomorrow. Agent Bianchi is just finishing up with our last interviewee now."

Angelica tipped her chin, and he came over to us. Angelica made a bubble of absolute silence. "There will be more people to interview. Did you get a list of enemies, friends, and relatives from her husband?"

"Yes. Do you want James and me on it straight away?"

"Yes, please. Lily and I are meeting Agent Floyd at the Cauldron and Broom shortly. When we're done, I'll message you and let you know."

"Why not meet him at HQ?"

"I don't want anything sabotaged. This one is important."

"But we're going to be interviewing some of the suspects and witnesses there." He ran a hand through his dark hair.

"I know, but you won't be discussing strategies and tactics or forensics. Protect those interviews with all the spells you can think of. We may as well make it as hard as possible for them. Even if the interviews lead nowhere, they'll think they're important. Have Beren on the lookout for those we know have signed up with the enemy. He can see if they increase their magic use at the time you're conducting the interviews. Actually, I'm going to call a meeting of all our agents. This could play into our hands. Are there any interviewees who've said they can come in this afternoon?"

"There was one woman." He looked at something on his notes phone app. "Irene Stokes. Her solicitor is available to see us at three."

The sly smile she gave was one I'd rarely seen. "Book them in."

I should know better, but I couldn't help it. "What are you planning?"

"You'll see, Lily. You'll see." Yep, I totally should've known better. "I'll see you in my study at the CH at two, Agent Blakesley."

He stared at her for a moment and gave a brief nod. There was no way he was asking her about her plans, being the professional he was. Looked like I was the only dumb one here… as usual. "Yes, Ma'am." He looked at me, and his gaze softened. "See you later. Stay safe."

I smiled. "You too."

"Okay, let's go. You can use my doorway, Lily."

I stepped through first, into a low-ceilinged and somewhat dark reception room, lit by a wall sconce and one small window set into a stone wall. The door to the pub dining area was open, probably because this was a witch-only pub, and public places didn't need security, at least during opening hours.

Not wanting to get in Angelica's way, I moved to the doorway. She came through and joined me. As we walked in and looked for a table for three, I asked, "How do they stop non-witches from coming in?"

She chose a table in the corner, next to a window. The ceilings were higher in here, but the thick mahogany beams made it feel just as suffocating as the reception room. Some people called it cosy and quaint, but low ceilings were not my friend. It was like being in a pretty coffin.

"There's a spell on the building. To non-witches, it appears rundown and closed."

My eyes widened. "But doesn't that use a crazy amount of magical energy? Who's keeping it going?"

"The witches who own it and work here give a little bit of magic every shift. They get paid extra for it too. If a witch is too weak to provide magic, they don't have to give any."

"Oh, wow. Interesting." Now that was answered, I picked the menu up off the table and perused it. "Yum. They have a great selection."

Angelica looked through hers. "Hmm, yes, dear." She looked at her watch. "We've got time for a proper lunch, so order whatever you want."

I smiled and melted into my seat. What a rarity to be able to eat a relaxing meal out, even if we were only here because of an investigation. We ordered our meal and drinks, and that's when Agent Floyd turned up. "Ma'am." He gave her a nod and shot one my way as well.

"This is Lily Bianchi. She contracts to us on occasion." I almost laughed. I wasn't far off being full-time the last few months. My dream to continue my professional photography business was fading by the day. Didn't matter how many things we survived, there was always something else.

I smiled. "Hi."

"Are you Agent Bianchi's sister?"

"That I am."

He nodded. "He's a good agent." He slipped his cumbersome lankiness into the seat opposite Ma'am and grabbed a menu off the table. I hoped Angelica was right and this guy was a *good agent* too, one who was on our side. If only one of my talents was to tell people's goodness through their aura.

After Agent Floyd ordered his lunch, Angelica pinned him with her gaze. She made a bubble of silence. "Did you find any signature?"

"No, but I found residue." Residue? He reached into his pocket and pulled out a glass vial. Angelica didn't reach for it, and he didn't offer it. There was probably nothing one could tell from the small amount of silverish powder in the container without doing sciency things on it. Could magic leave residue behind, or had someone done something to her in person? "Is it safe to take it back to the lab?"

"I think so. As long as you're with it the whole time. How long do you think you'll need?"

"A couple of hours."

Angelica glanced around before focussing on Floyd again. "What else did you find?"

"Entry wounds definitely signal that the strike came from above." He rubbed the back of his neck. "There should've been a hole in the ceiling."

"Yes, but there wasn't, so we have to figure out why." Angelica rested clasped hands on the table in front of her, as if she were sitting at the head of the conference-room table. Authority and control radiated from her. Even though our situation in general felt hopeless, her demeanour made me sit up straighter and believe we had a chance at both solving this crime and beating the crapheads who were out to get us. "One bolt or two? Did the magic branch off as the witnesses claimed?"

"The angle of the wounds indicate it did branch off. I did a magic simulation with the light and speed of the bolt but without the electricity. The spell has marked entry and exit points with a yellow dot roughly the same size as the victim's wounds. I magicked a test dummy from the lab and filmed the tests. It took three tries to get the angles right, but I'm pretty sure that's it." He unlocked his phone and brought up the video, which he held up for Ma'am and me to watch.

The bolt appeared to come from above and just to the back of her head. It hit the dummy's skull, part of the bolt going through it and another tentacle branching off to curve around its face and strike its heart. At the end of the video, he lay the dummy next to Mrs Fairchild's body and explained the comparison, not that there was much to explain. It was visually clear that both strikes were almost identical. Fascinating stuff.

"Can you airdrop that to me now, please?"

"Yes, Ma'am." His magic tickled my scalp—maybe a security spell?

"Thank you." Angelica checked her phone for the video, then put it in her inside jacket pocket, but just as our meals arrived, her phone rang. "Agent DuPree speaking." As the person on the other end spoke, she stared into the distance, her poker face activated. "We're working on it. Interviews are being undertaken as we speak." She paused again while the other person said something. "Yes, of course. I'll let you know as soon as we have something to tell you…. Okay…. Goodbye." Without saying anything else, she picked up her knife and fork and started eating.

Agent Floyd and I stared at Angelica, but that didn't spur her to say anything. Looked like that well was dry.

My stomach grumbled. "Okay, don't worry. I'll feed you now." Floyd gave me a weird look, and I smiled. "Yes, I'm a bit crazy, but aren't we all?" With that, I picked up my utensils and tucked into my steak. When my stomach spoke, I listened.

After lunch, Floyd and Angelica had another quick conversation; then he left. I made a bubble of silence. There was no way I could ask her anything before, but now we were alone, she was fair game. "Do you think you'll solve this one before everything goes to hell?"

She raised a brow. "You mean while we still have access to the bureau? Because you know, dear, I can't let this one slide, no matter what happens."

What was that supposed to mean? Surely she couldn't be in any more trouble with authority figures than she already was. "What if you can't solve it? And how are you supposed to do that without access to all those resources?"

She gave me a deadpan look. "I'm disappointed you even have to ask."

Was she bluffing, or did she have something up her sleeve? "Do you have a plan?"

Her head cocked to one side. "What do you think?"

CHAPTER 3

We all crammed into Angelica's country-house office: Will, Beren, Imani, Liv, Mum, Millicent, James, and me. Everyone stood, including Angelica, who was in between her chair and table facing us. Abby sat elegantly, front and centre, on the table as if she was the one who'd called us for the meeting. Ted, totally uninterested in what the humans were doing, was in his doggy bed in the room I'd chosen for Will and me as soon as I'd returned from lunch. Situated on the first floor, it held a king-size bed and overlooked the gorgeous walled garden and fields beyond.

"Thank you for all for attending. This afternoon, Will and James will be interviewing two of Mr and Mrs Fairchild's employees." It had originally been one woman, Irene Stokes, but looked as if another person had found a solicitor. Angelica addressed Liv and Mum, "Have you two let everyone know?"

Mum smiled. "Yes." She shared an excited look with Liv, then turned back to Angelica. "It was way too much fun spreading the rumours."

Right, so I was way out of the loop. "What rumours?"

Angelica gave Mum a nod, and Mum turned to me. "We let a few people know about the important case Angelica was working on, and that witnesses were being brought in this afternoon. I said it as though I was bragging—you know, I'm so awesome because I'm in the loop. We're hoping to draw our double agents out of the woodwork, so we can nab them for spying without letting on that we know about their association."

Imani shot Angelica a calculating look. "Is that so you can round them up without killing them?"

Angelica's proud smile broke through her serious visage. "Yes. I don't want to kill any of my agents if I can help it, even if they're traitors." Her smile twisted in disgust. "Maybe some of them are salvageable, but even if they're not, we can probably use them somehow, and if we can't, well, a life in gaol is their destiny." Use them? I didn't know how, since the directors could probably guess their double agents were compromised. The only way she could possibly use them would be to get more information about the directors and what they were up to. I supposed that was better than nothing.

"So, what's the plan for this afternoon?" Will asked.

Angelica looked at him. "You've all seen the list of traitors, so you'll know who to watch out for, but I'm also interested in anyone we don't know about who is acting suspiciously." She smoothed a hand down her lapel. "You and James will undertake the two interviews. While you're doing that, Lily and Agents Jawara, DuPree, and Bianchi"—her gaze cut to Millicent—"will be monitoring the complex for magic use." She looked at Liv and Mum, who stood next to each other. "Olivia and Kat will be manning the security videos to see where those traitor agents are. I doubt they'll be able to spy from their offices. With all our security, it's virtually impossible to implement a listening spell that will work from the first- or second-floor offices all the way down to the basement interview rooms." Angelica turned her gaze on me. "I want you to do a quick sweep of our interview rooms for spying devices before we begin. We need to make this as hard for our enemies as possible so we can catch them out when they scramble to listen in."

"Yes, Ma'am." Whilst I didn't necessarily want much to do with spy work, I'd rather be doing that than be here with Chadiot alone. So far, I'd managed to avoid the living room where he was caged.

Angelica's face relaxed somewhat, and her lips turned up enough that she seemed satisfied if not happy about things. Was she actually feeling it, or was this for our benefit? I'd never know. "Thank you, team. We'll arrive at the PIB in dribs and drabs over the next thirty minutes. Let them think we're trying to be subtle."

James took Mum and Liv first. The rest of us left over the next thirty minutes, arriving in ones and twos. I was with Will. As soon as we got to headquarters, he took me down to the interview rooms. As we stood in a hallway with four doors leading off it—two to the left and two to the right—he made a bubble of total silence. "We'll only use two of them, but best if you check them all out because you never know when circumstances will arise where we'll be forced into one rather than the other."

"Okay. Are you going to jam the PIB security cameras before we go in there?"

"Yep. Just give me a moment. Then you've got five minutes to do your thing. The guys on surveillance today are unknowns. They're not on our total-trust list." Will's magic tickled my scalp, and he mouthed a few words I couldn't quite catch. His magic stopped, and he gave me a thumbs up.

I nodded and opened the door to Interview Room 1. The

black plaque with white writing was positioned on a thick stainless steel door that was suited to a prison rather than a simple interview room, but when you were dealing with witches, the more security you had, the better. I looked at the door with my second sight. There were two spells on it, but I had no idea what they were. I opened it and went into the stark concrete-floored room, phone camera at the ready.

"Show me any bugging devices." Nothing came up immediately, but there were areas I couldn't see. I got on the floor on all fours to check under the three chairs and table. "Yep." I snapped photos of the two bugs, then took them off the underside of the table and underside of one chair. I wasn't sure what Will wanted to do with them, so I put them in my pocket.

The other rooms had similar devices. There weren't too many places to hide bugs when the only furniture was the interview chairs and tables. Except in one room, I found a grey bug in the corner on the floor. So small it was practically invisible to the human eye, my magic made it glow like a beacon. *Nice work, magic.*

When I was done, I exited and handed Will my stash. He drew magic and did something to the devices, then smiled. "I've disabled them. It wouldn't do to give them a front-row seat to our conversations. And thanks again for your indispensable service. Let's go." At the door to the exit, he magically reinstated the security video feed.

As he shut the door, I made a total bubble of silence. "Shouldn't you have done that while we were still standing in the spot, same as before?"

"No. I want them to think that we believe we're being sneaky. But I also didn't want them seeing what you were doing. We're making it hard for them but not impossible."

"Oookay. Fair enough."

"Make your way up to Angelica's office. I'm going to stay down here and wait for James so we can go through the questions I want to ask. We can't forget that we're also trying to catch a killer."

I looked to the sky and found a stark white ceiling. "Yes, I haven't forgotten. It seems that's all we do lately. Sorry if that sounds whiney, but it would be nice to have a holiday, especially as the last one didn't go as planned." A pang for Sydney sliced me in the heart. I didn't often get homesick, but it did sneak up on me from time to time.

Will cocked his head to the side and pulled me to him. "Once we're free of the directors and their goonies, why don't we get married over there? We'll make it a group holiday with everyone." Was he reading my mind? I checked my mind shield. Nope. He just knew me that well.

Despite everything we were dealing with, I grinned. "That would be awesome. Do you really mean it?"

"Why wouldn't I? The more I think about it, the more I think it's a brilliant idea. But you know I'm always having those." He winked.

I laughed. "You are. Be warned that I'm going to hold you to that. Maybe we should start planning?"

His love-filled smile warmed my belly. "And this is why we make a great team—we're both awesome at the brilliant ideas." He gave me a steamy kiss, then sent me on my way with a feeling that we could do this. We were going to live long enough to get married, and I'd finally get to show him where I grew up. They were excellent incentives to push through the crap.

With renewed motivation, I strode to Angelica's office. "Gus, what are you doing here?" He was standing with his back to Ma'am's closed outer-office door.

"Personal security on her offices. When she's in, I stand out here, and when she's out, I'm in there making sure no one trespasses."

"Doesn't she have spells for that?"

"Yes, but she wants to make sure, if you know what I mean." He tapped his nose with his index finger, which was wrapped in a bandage.

"What happened to your finger, and why didn't you ask Beren to heal it?"

He looked at said digit. "My dog caught a squirrel, and I was saving it… the squirrel not the dog. And the damn thing bit me. Ungrateful rodent. Next time I won't bother. I had to go get stitches and a tetanus shot."

I wasn't sure if Beren could magic something against tetanus. Magic skills were more about fixing what was already broken than preventing stuff. "Oh, that's no good. I can have a word to your squirrels for you if you want. In fact, I'm trying to recruit some for my squirrel army, and a bitey squirrel would be awesome."

He looked at me as if I'd just told him I ate my own toenails. "Are you pulling my leg?"

"Not at all. I'm deadly serious. Did you know that the American and Russian navies use dolphins, sea lions, and orcas as soldiers?"

He laughed. "Stop, Miss Lily. Now I know you're being silly."

"Google it." I smiled and knocked on the door. I'd stumbled upon that information randomly, and yay that I'd gotten to shock someone with it.

"Come in," rang out from inside.

I opened the door and turned to Gus. "See you on my way out." He nodded slowly, possibly still processing all the information bombs I'd just dropped on him. Hmm, would it be possible to recruit different animals, not just squirrels? Dogs, cats, and birds could do damage, but then again, did I want to put their cute little lives at risk? The one good thing would be that their intervention would be unexpected. Maybe we could use them to surprise people rather than full-on attack them, which would mean they would be less likely to be harmed by the surprised person. It would give us time to mount a magical attack. I'd have to speak to Abby and Ted and see what they thought. I smiled. This could work.

"Lily? Earth to Lily, come in, Lily." Imani's voice broke through my inner ramblings.

I blinked and realised I was standing in the doorway from the outer office to the inner office. Imani, Angelica, Millicent, and Beren watched me, amused smiles on their faces. "Oops. Sorry. Just thinking about how I can expand my squirrel army to include other animal types."

Angelica chuckled and shook her head. "At the risk of missing out on your brilliant plan, I'm not going to ask you about it. How did things go with Will?"

Argh. Why did no one applaud my fantastic ideas until I'd proven they were good? Why did no one have vision? "Fine. We got them all. He's holding onto them for now."

"Good." Her magic tingled my scalp, and her palm filled with little skin-coloured earpieces. She handed one to each person. "These will give you a magically protected link directly to either Olivia or Kat. They'll give you instructions. I'll be participating with you." Her magic pinged my scalp again, and a pair of handcuffs appeared in her hand. She looked at me. "These are for you, Lily."

My eyes widened, and goosebumps skittered along my arms. "You can't expect me to arrest anyone. I'm not an agent. Surely I can't legally use those. And I've had no practice." Expecting me to overpower a trained witch agent without accidentally killing them with a lightning bolt was too much to ask, not to mention, even if I managed to subdue them without murdering them, I'd probably end up handcuffing myself with their help. This would not end well.

Imani smirked and slapped me on the back. "You'll be fine, love. Just don't kill anyone."

I looked at her. "You're joking, right? That's what I do. I smite people down. All. The. Time. I have no self-control when I panic."

Angelica's confident gaze found me. "That's why I'm going to teach you a new spell. If you find someone channelling magic, you're to cast a freeze spell, which you already know. Do it first and ask questions later. Once they're frozen, you can check their aura for spell signatures. While you're doing that, you can take a snapshot magically with your phone that will be programmed to go directly to my phone app. Millicent's father worked on this for a couple of weeks, and I dare say he's done an outstanding job. The image will come to my phone, and we can use it for evidence later. Once you've done that—and only when you've done that—can you put the cuffs on them and cut off their magic. When that happens, we'll lose the signature and our evidence."

I stared at her, my brain processing.

Beren chuckled. "Hey, Lily's speechless. This can't be right. The apocalypse is coming. Everyone, run!" But everyone didn't run—they laughed.

Finally, my brain and mouth connected. "Ha ha, very funny. I'm not happy about the pressure to do this right, but I can handle it. God knows I've pulled off stuff that was way more complicated." I folded my arms and gave a firm nod. Hopefully my bravado was fooling them because it wasn't fooling me.

Millicent gave me a reassuring smile. "That's the spirit, Lily. We all have complete faith in you."

"Are you sure we shouldn't call Sarah and Lavender and get them to come and help?" Safety in numbers and all that.

Angelica shook her head. "They don't have time. They're working on other things. Now, let me show you that spell." Angelica demonstrated it a couple of times. I thought it through, then asked her to show me again, which she did. "Now, let's see you do it, dear."

Angelica cast a spell—I had no idea what it was. She could've created a cake at home for all I knew. I cast my freeze spell, then the first part of the spell she'd just shown me. My mouth dropped open as two spell sigils appeared in her aura. "Wow, okay." Once I'd done that, I pointed my phone camera at it, said a single word while taking a photo, and imagined the sigils appearing on Angelica's phone, "Click." At least it was a word I couldn't forget.

Angelica dropped her magic, and her phone dinged. She opened her app, looked at me, then smiled. "Nice work, dear. Perfect execution."

I couldn't help but return the smile as warmth bloomed in my chest. "Thank you." Now I just had to get it right in the field and hope my freeze spell wasn't too hard to hold at the same time. The stronger the witch I was constricting, the harder a freeze spell was to maintain.

"Now, Agent Jawara, I want you on the ground floor north wing. That's within the spell radius. Any level above that, I don't think they'd manage it." Angelica looked at Beren. "You take B2 west." The interview rooms were on B1, so that made sense. "Lily, I want you on B1 in a storeroom near the interview rooms. If you sense any magic, go and investigate. Just grab a laptop still in its box from the storeroom. You can pretend you're getting it because your old one broke."

"Won't they wonder why I didn't magic it to myself?"

"No, dear. We were sick of agents stealing the more

expensive office equipment, so we've spelled that storeroom. It's by approval only. The agent gets a special code that opens the door, and a stock take is magically done as soon as they leave the room. Your code is 214489. Think you can remember it?"

"No." I put it in my phone. Imani and Angelica shared a look, like, *maybe it's a good idea she's not an agent.* I wasn't going to argue with that sentiment. I smiled. "At least I know my limitations."

Angelica's brow rose, but she said nothing. "Are we all clear on what we have to do?" Thankfully, her gaze left me and travelled over everyone else.

We all nodded, and Beren said, "Yes, Ma'am." He was always so polite.

As I left the office, I slid the earpiece into my ear. "Bye, Gus."

"Bye, Miss Lily. Stay safe."

I smiled. "You too. And, seriously, ask Beren to heal that finger." He'd had his tetanus shot, so the rest should be good to heal by witch powers. Gus gave a nod, but I didn't trust him. Maybe he didn't want to bother B, since he was so busy? Oh well. Not my circus, not my monkeys.

Imani and Beren caught up to me. Imani made a bubble of silence. "Hey, we're going in the same direction. Mind if we join you?"

"Of course not."

Beren piped up. "Of course we can't join you, or of course you don't mind?" He waggled his brows.

"Ha ha, it was number two, but now I'm reconsidering."

We reached the lift, and I pressed the button. Imani slipped the earpiece into her ear. "Have you tried yours yet, Lily?"

"No."

"Best test it before we get in the lift. If there's a problem, you can go back and get another one."

"Good idea. Can you drop the BOS?"

"Certainly, love."

Once Imani did that, I spoke into the earpiece quietly. "Testing, testing, this is Lily. Please respond."

There wasn't even a crackle before a voice responded. "Hey, Lily. It's Liv. I'll be your contact today."

"Nice." They probably hadn't given me my mother because she would have freaked out on me if she'd heard me in a dangerous situation. "Okay, well, I'll go now—about to get in the lift. I'll let you know when I'm in my hiding spot."

"Okay. Thanks. Be careful."

"I will. Thanks. Bye." The lift doors opened as Imani and Beren were saying goodbye to my mother. "All working?"

Beren nodded. "Yep. Yours?"

"Yep."

Imani pressed all the buttons we needed. "Good. We're all set." When the lift stopped on the ground floor, she got out. "Good luck." And then she was gone. I pressed the Close Door button because I couldn't wait for the lift to get its act together. I'm sure I only saved a few seconds, but waiting patiently was impossible in a lift. I had no idea why—it just was.

The lift stopped on B1. "Stay safe, B."

"You too." He gave me a smile. "We got this, as we have so many times before."

I smiled, ignoring the way my gut churned. "We do. See you later." The doors opened, and off I got. I made my way towards the interview rooms, but at a T-intersection turned right instead of left. Not far from there, I stopped well short at a door that had a keypad on the wall next to it. A small sign said Store 1. I brought up the code on my phone and punched it in. The door clicked. I pushed it open, turned on the light just inside the door, and entered, then shut the door behind me.

The room wasn't small. At around twenty-five feet by twenty-five feet, it was the size of a four-car garage. Black metal shelving ran from where I stood to the back wall, and there were numerous rows. Signs hanging from the ceiling, like in a supermarket, gave an indication of what was in each row. I searched for the one that said computers. I found it in a row that was also labelled Printers, Ink Cartridges, Memory Sticks, Headphones, Webcams. Looked like they had everything. Imagine walking into an office-supply store and being able to take whatever you wanted. That's what this felt like. I smiled and had to remind myself that I wasn't actually allowed to take whatever I wanted. Bummer. It was like waking from a dream where I was in a chocolate shop and being able to grab all the incredible deliciousness for free. Total disappointment.

I looked at the boxes on the shelves. The smaller ones were higher up. Gah, I'd need a ladder, but there wasn't one in here from what I could see. Hmm, how dangerous would it be to climb up there? It was only one shelf higher than I could reach. Then I shut my eyes. *Idiot*. I'd been here for over a year now; surely I should be used to witch ways by now?

Magic flowed into me, and I said, "Please send the laptop I'm looking at into my hands." It disappeared from the shelf and appeared in my hands. I grinned. Magic was awesome.

Now I just had to wait. But what if one of our bad agents had seen me go in here because they had spying devices in the hallway or some kind of access to the security video system? Would they wonder why I was in here so long? Doh. Maybe I should've waited in the toilet. There was probably a toilet near here. I imagined that nervous crims would ask for a toilet break on occasion, especially if the interview became hours upon hours of interrogation.

I made a bubble of absolute silence and spoke to Liv. "Hey, is there a toilet near this storeroom? I'm worried our cover might be blown if someone saw me come in but not out. This is a weird place to spend more than five to ten minutes."

"Oh, good point. Let me just bring up a map. Hang on a sec." I waited for a minute, on alert for noises outside the room or for magic being drawn. "Yes, there's a toilet. If you go out of that storeroom and turn left, the end of the hallway has a door. That door leads to separate male and female toilets. It's further from the interview rooms though."

"Okay, thanks. Can you talk to Ma'am? I'd text her, but she might have her phone on silent and not vibrate."

"Yes, I can. I'll ask her if that's a good idea or whether you should stay put."

"Thanks." While I waited, I went to the door and sat on the floor next to it, my back against the wall. I listened intently. Nothing. I looked at my phone. Dead on three o'clock. Will and James should be in an interview room, getting settled to begin with the first suspect or witness. I wasn't sure what they were calling them. Maybe they were both?

"Lily?"

"Yep. Still here."

"Ma'am says it shouldn't make much difference if you're in there, but she's considered the location of the toilets, and you might end up being in there with them. She's suggested you stay where you are. If you sense magic, that's most likely where it will be coming from. There are a couple of offices on the other side of the interview rooms too. They're the likely places, oh and the storeroom next to yours, but she checked, and no one has been given a code for a couple of days, so they probably won't go there."

"Okay, thanks. I'll stay put then. Bye." At least whatever happened wouldn't be on my head if I'd blown my cover by staying here.

I tapped my foot. It might be a long wait. If no one tried anything on this level and the interviews went for hours, I'd be stuck here the whole time for nothing. Yes, I was supposed to be concentrating, but stuff it. I brought up my reading app and got back to the thriller I was a third of the way through. I could still listen and feel for magic while I entertained myself. Who said staking out basement level one had to be mind-numbingly boring?

Twenty minutes later, I was glad I had a book to read. I'd sensed, and my earpiece had been quiet. Hopefully Beren and Imani had figured out how nothing to entertain themselves too. They'd had way more practice than me, though. Maybe they were good at waiting and staring into space?

After another five minutes, my scalp prickled. I clicked my phone screen, making it dark, and slipped it into my pocket. I whispered into my coms, "I can feel magic. It's not Will's or James's." The two people I knew were nearby.

Liv was quick to answer. "Can you tell where it's coming from?"

I stood and shook out my legs. I opened the door and walked out, as if there was nothing suspicious about me being here. All my concentration was on the magic, which vibrated more strongly now I was out in the hall. And surprise, surprise, it was coming from the end of the hallway where the toilets were.

I walked casually, holding the computer and half smiling, as if I was excited about my new toy. I didn't try and be quiet —I opened the door normally, making sure not to hold my magic. If it was one of our bad guys channelling magic, they'd be on alert for someone else doing the same. The door led to a small hallway with two doors—one that said Women, the other Men. Stopping, I focussed on which door I should go into. Crap. The person was in the men's toilet. How was I supposed to walk in there without drawing attention to myself?

Oh well, I could pretend I made a mistake. Hopefully they were in a cubicle. I crossed my fingers that no one was at a trough as I opened the door. Ew, the stench was gross. Even with magic, they couldn't manage to keep the toilets stink free? I stared at the floor. Imagine all the invisible wee germs. How many men missed or dribbled the last little bit on the floor, then walked it around the place? I shuddered. Where was the ability to levitate when you needed it?

At least I hadn't surprised anyone—the main area was empty. Of the two cubicles, one was occupied. I bent and looked across the room to the space under the toilet door. Black boots and black pants. Definitely an agent.

I entered the cubicle next to him and fiddled the lock on the door for authenticity, but I didn't actually lock it—I might need a speedy exit.

His magic gave off nervousness and competence. He was likely good at his job and magic but was worried about getting caught. Maybe he was also a nervous personality? I quietly put the seat down and sat on it. Hmm, would he think it was weird that I wasn't making any tinkling noises? Damn it.

I made a noise like I was straining to get a number two out. I made sure it was loud and deep, like a man would sound. Authenticity was key. There was no break in the guy's magic flow. So far, he wasn't worried about me. Good. But how was I going to cast a freeze spell on him? I needed to be looking at him while I did it. I grunted again and groaned like I had a stomach ache. I almost went too far and said how bad my stomach ache was, then remembered my voice would give me away. Doh.

How was I going to do this? If I kicked the door open, I might hurt him, but then again, he was likely one of the bad guys, so what did it matter? I went over the freeze spell in my head without drawing my magic, made a last, "Eeeeeurgh," and spun the toilet paper roll around the holder so it made a noise. As I gave time for wiping, his magic grew stronger. Was he having trouble hearing anything? I hoped so.

I stood and lifted the toilet lid slightly before letting it drop, as if I'd only just shut it, then flushed. This was it. The moment of truth. I quietly took out the handcuffs jammed in my jacket pocket and left the cubicle. I turned the tap on so he'd think I was washing my hands—hopefully that wouldn't be a dead giveaway that I wasn't a man, ha ha—then tiptoed to his cubicle.

I'm a ninja. I got this.

Here goes nothing.

I lifted my knee as high as it would go, my leg bent, foot ready to extend. I took a deep breath, my heart racing. *Please work.* If I stuffed this up, I'd be in trouble because he was already sworn to the directors. I had no doubt he knew about the price on my head. This could end very badly.

I kicked my foot out as hard as I could, my toes curled back, and at the same time, I drew my magic. Oh my God, what if he was wearing a return to sender? Crap. Why hadn't we thought about that? Maybe because Angelica figured he wouldn't be expecting to be caught. Whatever the reason, it was all my problem now.

Just do it, Lily. You'll figure it out. My inner voice was such a bad influence. It was going to get me killed one of these days.

My foot connected with the cubicle door, and what little resistance the small lock had gave way. The door flew inwards, smashing into the man's knee. Sitting on the toilet, his head jerked up, and the salt-and-pepper-haired forty-something-year-old stared at me in shock. His magic faltered. I made sure he wasn't wearing a return to sender, then let my freeze spell fly.

Please work.

It hit him. Yes!

I cast the next spell under his fearful hazel stare. His aura was lit with two spells. I lifted my phone and took a picture. "Click." It would automatically upload to Ma'am's phone, and that was that. Well, except for one more thing.

The gap in the door wasn't huge since the agent's knee was in my way, but it was big enough for me to squeeze through. His hands were in front of him, and getting the cuffs on would be too difficult if I had to jam his arms behind his back, so I slipped one bracelet on one wrist. *Click.* I moved his other hand closer to its brother and slipped the other bracelet on. *Click.* "No more magic for you, mister." I wasn't game to take the freeze spell off yet, even though the drain of it meant I'd be exhausted within twenty minutes. He was still bigger and stronger than me, and I could just see him knocking me out and running away if I didn't use magic on him.

He couldn't use his mouth to protest, but his eyes conveyed his anger. He might think I was just some random crazy person. Did he realise why he'd been targeted? Unless he wasn't one of the double agents. Hmm, that would be funny. He did look familiar though—I'd seen the list of compromised agents with names and photos, but there were so many, I couldn't be sure I didn't just recognise him from passing him in the corridor. "Wait here one moment." I moved his knees to the side, opened the door all the way, and let the door rest against him again. I didn't want the door closed, just in case he did something sneaky when I came back. If the door had shut, I'd know something was off.

I left the bathroom and spoke into my earpiece. "Liv, can you find out if those spells are spying ones?"

I'd forgotten that I wasn't really alone while doing all that. It had just felt like it. "Just a moment. Also, great going-to-the-toilet noises. It was super authentic." She giggled.

I grinned. "Ha, thanks. I'm a master at undercover work."

After a minute, she responded. "Yep. He's definitely up to no good. Will and James will join you in a moment. We're getting them to pause the interview for a couple of minutes so they can lock your guy up."

"Okay, thanks." I went back into the bathroom, hoping no one had stolen the guy out from under my nose. Phew, he was still there. I probably shouldn't have left him alone, but I didn't want him hearing anything, and with the freeze spell sapping my energy, I didn't want to add to it. I leaned my backside against the handbasin and tapped my foot while I waited.

Finally, Will strode through the door. His gaze found me, then moved to my captive. James walked in and joined Will at the cubicle. James turned and looked at me. "Nice work. We'll take it from here."

Will's poker face settled into place. "Lily, you can drop that freeze spell."

The relief when I cut off my magic was immense. It was like I'd been jogging, and all of a sudden, I'd been resting for two minutes and gotten my breath back. "Ooh, that's much better."

He gave me a small smile. "Can you just move over there?" He nodded to the far corner, further along from where I stood.

"Ah, sure." Were they going to drag him out and beat him up? That wasn't normally their style, but this guy was a traitor, the worst of the worst. I got out of the way.

Will made a doorway as James yanked the guy off his

throne. "What are you doing? Where are you taking me? I haven't done anything. Are you all insane?"

"Agent Paul, save your breath." James glared at him. "You're not fooling anyone." James dragged the guy towards the doorway.

"You're not taking me anywhere. I demand to see Ma'am and a lawyer." He fought against my brother's hold. There was no way it was safe to send him through a doorway like that. He would hit the sides, and he might even hurt James in the process.

James stood behind him and dug his fingers into Agent Paul's upper arms. "Are you going to go quietly, or am I going to have to do it the hard way?"

Agent Paul growled and swore at my brother, telling him exactly what he thought about that.

James's smile was predatory. I'd never seen him so, well, enjoying punishing someone. "You asked for it." He slid his arm around the front of Agent Paul's throat until he was gripping his own bicep, creating a tight headlock. James brought his other hand to the back of the agent's head and rested his forehead against the back of it. He pushed the agent's head forward and held that position until the guy fainted.

Will smiled. "Nice work. Do you need any help dragging him through?"

"Nah, I got this. Thanks for asking." James dragged the agent through the doorway and disappeared.

Will followed. "See you later, Lily."

"Um, bye."

And that was that. One traitor down. Now we just had to get the rest.

CHAPTER 4

After checking in with Liv, I wandered the B1 corridors. I hadn't felt any other magic, even when the guys were back interviewing, so eventually I made it back to my hidey-hole. Two hours later when I was onto my next book, Liv's voice came through my earbud. "Meeting where the last meeting was."

"Yep. Roger that. Do you need a lift?"

"I'm fine. B is going to take your mother and me."

"Cool. See you there soon." I slowly unfurled to standing from the uncomfortable concrete. My hips screamed at me to take it easy, and my bottom was numb. I shook my legs one at a time and did a little dance thing. Yay for getting out of this place. I turned off the light and illuminated everything with my phone before making my doorway and stepping through to the country-house reception room.

I opened the door and went in, locking it behind me. Voices came from the living room, and one of them was Imani's. I drew magic—who knew what I'd encounter with Chadiot there.

It was even worse than I thought.

The cages had multiplied. Three of the magically enhanced structures took up space in the living room. Chadiot's cage was back to the original smaller one. Two other identical cages, spaced ten feet apart, sat at the far end of the room. Each cage was far enough from the others that no one could touch each other, assuming the forcefield failed and they could reach their arms out.

Agent Paul was in one, and a female agent was in another. I blinked. She was an agent I'd met a couple of times who'd seemed really nice. I searched my brain, trying to picture the list Angelica had given us of names with photos of the double agents. Finally, her name came to me—Agent Patty Francis. She was in her thirties, had a straight blonde bob and sparkling blue eyes. Her friendly demeanour in the past had me thinking she was super lovely. How disappointing—both because I'd thought she was nice, and because my good-person radar was so far off it made men's aim at the toilet seem accurate. Argh, being in that men's bathroom had scarred me for life.

Beren stood next to her cage, his arms folded. "Well, you should've thought of that before you tried spying." I had no idea of their history, but his grim face was evidence that she'd been someone he'd trusted and least expected. He would've noticed her on the list, but seeing her do the wrong thing in person was probably still a punch to the gut.

Ma'am came through the door. When she had that superior, totally-in-control look, she was all Ma'am and not Angelica. I'd gotten comfortable with Angelica, but Ma'am still scared me sometimes.

She sized up the cages' occupants. Chadiot stood there, arms folded, a scowl in place, possibly more worried than ever that he was never going to be rescued. Ma'am gave him a smirk, then approached the other cages. Agents Carl Paul and Patty Francis were both on our list of compromised agents. It was great that we'd caught them, but there were still so many left. Did they each know the other was a double agent? Also, how many did Ma'am plan on storing here?

Ma'am had replaced her smirk with an ominous frown. She drew a trickle of power, and menace poured off her. Huh, you learned something new every day. I knew why she appeared scarier, but the agents who couldn't sense magic would have to assume, or maybe they wouldn't twig. She probably didn't do it to witches who could see what she was doing. It would likely spoil the effect.

She targeted Agent Paul first. He stood straight, arms folded, as if he didn't have a care in the world, but his poker face didn't quite cut it, and I could see the sheen of dread in his eyes. Did he fear Angelica, or what she might make him say? No doubt, he'd sworn on his life and was currently at risk of losing it.

Ma'am stopped a few inches from the cage. Her stern voice cut through the silence. "Care to tell me why you were attempting to spy on our suspect interviews?"

He was quick to answer, some of the fear receding. I wasn't sure if Angelica wanted them to know we knew. I glanced at Chad. Had he told them, or had Angelica spelled him silent on the subject? "I wasn't." He glared at me. "I don't know what that amateur told you, but that wasn't what I was doing." I knew it was sour grapes that I'd surprised him, but the insult still irked. How dare he! He was the criminal in all this, not me. At least his deflection would never work.

"So, what were you doing, then?"

"That's none of your business." He took a step back, and his eyes widened, likely because he remembered he was in a cage that could electrocute him.

Angelica's brow rose. "You were on PIB time, not your lunch hour. It *is* my business." She smiled, and there wasn't an ounce of kindness in it. "But I'll let it go for now because I know the truth. I'm also not ready to force the issue… yet." He paled at that. She could mean anything, and he'd have to wait to find out whether she was talking about this incident or the double-agent thing.

She turned to Agent Francis. The woman's shoulders drooped, but then she drew them up and back and held herself tall. Had she almost caved already? I would've thought she'd be stronger than that. "And what have you got to say for yourself, Agent Francis? Why were you spying on those interviews?"

The look on the woman's face was in between shame and fear. Her words didn't match the apologetic expression on her face. "I'm admitting to nothing."

Angelica threw up her poker face faster than a bank-counter security screen deploying. What did it mean? "I see."

"You can't keep us locked up. This is illegal!" Agent Paul had no shame, apparently.

I smiled. "Aw, you poor, poor, hard done by man." He glowered at me. "I may be an amateur, but I put your behind in jail. Embarrassed much?"

"You're not even an agent. What are you doing wearing our uniform? You're the embarrassment." It was a surprise when he didn't stick his tongue out like a four-year-old.

"I'm not technically an agent, but I have more loyalty to the PIB in one nostril hair than you do in your whole body. You should be ashamed, spying on an interview, and for what? Did the murderer pay you?" I had no idea where I was going with this, but Angelica was letting me have at it. She must think I might knock something loose.

"Loyalty? You have no clue what you're talking about.

When an organisation asks everything of you and you give that and more, yet you're still treated like dirt, that's loyalty. You've had preferential treatment since you arrived. And I know why."

"Tell me about it," Chad muttered from his cage. He lounged in his comfortable armchair and sighed. He had it easy, being looked after by Angelica. Okay, so he was locked in a cage like an animal, but still. At least he wasn't dead.

Angelica looked at me and must've decided I actually wasn't going anywhere with it. You won some; you lost some. "Enough! I'll be back later. I don't have time for lies. You've both disappointed me beyond measure." Her tone held real heat. Chad, she couldn't care less about, but these two agents had trained under her and worked for her. She knew them well, but maybe not as well as she thought. The disappointment she spoke of was likely felt bone deep. She looked at Imani, then Beren, then me. "Time to go. My study, please."

As we entered the hallway, Will, James, Millicent, Liv, and Mum strolled out of the reception room. Perfect timing. Angelica looked at them. "Follow me."

Once we were all in her study, Beren shut the door, and Angelica made a bubble of silence. "I'm going to make the first part of this quick. We'll hold those traitors indefinitely. I don't have time to interrogate them properly right now, so we'll save it for later. I'm afraid it means we'll have to take time guarding them. Those two are a heck of a lot smarter than Chadiot." I smiled, happy that my name for him had caught on. Angelica sat down and looked up at James. "The second piece of business is the murder case. What did you find out, Agent Bianchi? Where are we at with those two employees?"

"I asked both of them if they killed her, and they both answered no. My talent tells me that's correct. When I asked if they liked her, they both said of course. My talent told me they lied. My takeaway from the interviews is that those two, unless they have a counter-talent for lying and believing their own bull, didn't kill her. I'd also hazard a guess and say that the victim wasn't much liked at work. We're speaking to her husband and family tomorrow, so we'll know more. She has an ex-husband and children from that marriage that we're interviewing."

"If no one likes her," I asked, "why is her cousin desperate to get to the bottom of it? Even if your friend was close to Mrs Fairchild's mother, he could've stayed out of it."

Angelica shrugged. "Maybe they got on well? He might also just want the scandal dealt with quickly before it attaches itself to him. Phillip is a decent fellow, but he is a politician at heart. One never can trust their motives." She licked her bottom lip. Did she know more than she was letting on?

At least my photos made more sense. "Those photos I took showed her chewing out people or spying on them. I guess that confirms she wasn't very nice to her staff. I also overheard a couple of the staff talking about her and saying it was karma."

Angelica raised a brow. "When we're done here, tell James which office they were in, and I'll have him follow it up."

"Okay."

James looked at Angelica. "Did Floyd find anything?"

"Yes, as a matter of fact. He's analysing it as we speak. There was spell residue on the body."

Will pursed his lips. "That's interesting. Did you find any other evidence upstairs?"

"I'm afraid not." Angelica frowned. "Whoever did it, didn't do it from there. They've either cast a set-and-wait spell, or they've made a doorway, ducked in and cast the spell, then ducked out again."

James scrunched his eyes shut, then opened them again. "I asked Jasmin if she saw what happened, and she said just that

Mrs Fairchild was struck. I should've asked if she saw who did it. Damn. I didn't think of it."

Will put a hand on James's shoulder. "Don't stress. We'll ask Jasmin tomorrow. Call her now and get her to set up another time with her solicitor."

James looked at Will, a "yeah right" expression on his face. "It might take days to get her to come back. Not only was she annoyed at being summoned in the first place, she was offended that we suspected her… like that wasn't the most obvious scenario. It could take a while to get to the bottom of that."

Angelica waved a hand in the air. "When are you interviewing the man who was in the room? Just ask him."

James answered, "He hasn't confirmed. Hopefully this week."

Angelica gave a nod. "Great. Now, let's move on. I want to get this solved ASAP so we can get back to some of the other cases." She pressed her lips together in a rare show of frustration. "Damn those greedy, ethically challenged directors." Her phone rang. "Angelica DuPree speaking." Whoever was on the other end was speaking loudly and quickly—a male. "Slow down. I can't understand what you're saying." After a minute or so, Angelica shut her eyes and rubbed her temples with the thumb and ring finger of one hand. She opened her eyes. "Yes. I'll have someone there straight away to take a statement. Goodbye."

We all stared at her, waiting for the news. I guess crimes didn't stop happening just because we didn't have time to deal with them. What was it going to be like when the PIB wasn't in the UK any more? Nausea swished in my belly. How long would it take for witch-perpetrated chaos to unfold?

Angelica put her phone on her desk. "Will, I want you and Lily to go and talk to Mr Fairchild. He's just received a phone call telling him he'll be next." Why was she sending me? It wasn't as if any photos would need to be taken. Angelica looked at Beren and Imani. "I want you two on the Jamison case. There's not much you can do on this one for today, and we're so close to a result. The labs should be back. If we can tie that up, I'd feel a lot better."

"Yes, Ma'am," they answered. They went out into the hallway to make their doorways and left.

Ma'am turned to James. "We'll take Liv and Kat back to headquarters, then plan, go over where we're at with those other cases. This damn murder has thrown everything out of whack, and we can't ignore it."

"What about me?" Millicent asked.

"You go grab your daughter, dear, and I'll see you at dinner tonight. One of us needs to be fresh, and I'm sure your parents could use a break from looking after the little one."

Millicent smiled. She would be missing Annabelle too. As much as Mill loved her work, we'd been through so many manic periods of overtime that her parents saw her daughter more than she did. "Thanks. I'll see you later." The room wasn't as crowded now, so she made her doorway in the study and walked through.

Will looked at Angelica. "Are we interviewing him at work?"

"No. He went home. I have the new coordinates. Here." Her magic tingled my scalp, and the digits appeared in my head. "Come back here when you're done, and we'll have a dinner meeting tonight, just the five of us." I guessed she meant James and Millicent since we were all staying here for the foreseeable future. It had been years since I'd lived with my brother. This was going to be kind of fun… well, as much fun as you could have while having a price on your head.

"Why am I going?" I had to ask, just in case I was

expected to do something and I didn't realise, then got into trouble.

"You're going so we can look like we're taking it extremely seriously. We are, of course, but if we send one agent, Mr Fairchild may think we're not giving him enough attention. We also might need your skills to see if anyone's been stalking his house. I think a few photos around the place would be good. You might even ask a few questions about Mrs Fairchild. See if you can confirm they were as happy together as he told your brother earlier."

James's forehead furrowed. "My talent told me he was mainly telling the truth. Obviously, couples have their problems, but overall, I got the impression that they were happy enough. There was certainly nothing that raised alarm bells."

"Nevertheless, dear, I want to make sure. Our talents don't always perform perfectly."

At least I knew what I was doing. "Okay, will do."

Will looked at me. "Ready?"

"Yep."

"See you there in a jiff."

I waited a few seconds after he stepped through his doorway to make mine. Then I joined him. Hopefully this would be an uneventful interview. Today had been exciting enough, thank you very much. Was it really only this morning Angelica's house had been attacked? It felt like a week ago. I crossed my fingers that the rest of the day didn't follow suit.

CHAPTER 5

Will and I sat next to each other on a four-seater fabric lounge in an opulent and gaudily decorated room that had everything from gold-coloured columns to a life-size statue of Venus. It was apparent the owners were filthy rich and that money didn't buy you style.

The lounge was oversized and comfortable, but the fabric print was… unusual. That would be the polite word for the white background peppered with bunches of green and purple grapes. I'd never seen anything like it. "Did your wife have this specially made?" I jammed my lips together. Oops. I probably wasn't supposed to say anything. This was Will's interview. The man himself glared at me in warning.

Mr Fairchild, seated in an armchair bearing the same unfortunate fabric, sniffled, and a whimsical smile settled on his face. "Yes. My darling loved decorating this place. She was wonderfully artistic, and this is one of her own designs. We have the matching curtains in our bedroom." I could picture their room. It probably had a huge bed shaped like a pineapple or something. If I had to name the style, I'd call it fruity. I bit my lip so I wouldn't smile. *Bad Lily.*

Will had a pen and pad out. "Mr Fairchild, can you tell me the person's exact words? Recall the conversation from start to finish as best as you can."

He swallowed and nodded. "Okay. Um…. He said, 'Is this Mr Fairchild,' and I said yes. He said, 'You know what happened to your wife? Well, you're next.' And that was it. He hung up." He scrubbed a hand over his face. "And before you ask, I didn't recognise the voice, and I don't know who'd hate us enough to kill both of us. I mean, plenty of women were jealous of my Adelaide, but did they hate her enough to kill her? I don't think so. And I have no enemies… at least none I'd consider murderers. I told you and that other agent this already."

Will looked at the ground, probably trying to compose himself. This guy wasn't being helpful for someone who had his life on the line. And boy, did he overestimate his judgement when it came to figuring out who wanted to kill him. Will raised his head and looked at Mr Fairchild. "I think you can leave that assessment up to us, Mr Fairchild. It's what we get paid for." He waited for the man's nod before continuing. "Apart from the business rivals you mentioned in our previous conversation, are there any people in your social circles who were more jealous than others of your wife, or you, for that matter?"

Mr Fairchild scratched behind his ear. "Well, there was one couple, Marie and Arnold Schwartzhausen. He's a German mogul, runs a financial services company in Switzerland, Germany, and Belgium. He's rich, but not as rich as me. His wife was always trying to one-up Addie. If Addie got a five-carat diamond ring, Marie had to get a six-carat one. That kind of thing. The last time they were here for an event, Marie threw a glass of red wine over Addie. It was quite the scene. Terrible. Anyway, my wife told her to leave and never come back. Addie's also the head of a high-profile charity group—Responsive Impassioned Caring Humanitarians—RICH. After that incident, she cut Marie from the group. Marie has been screaming about it ever since." He chuckled. "Her husband's also jealous of my rare classic Ferrari. He can't one-up me because there aren't any that are more desirable. I also have the latest one on order. There are a finite number produced, and I think he missed out on that too." He seemed rather pleased with himself. It was pathetic when you were so rich that your fun in life was to rub another rich person's face in what you had that they didn't. I shook my head. It was another world entirely.

Will did well to keep a neutral expression. "How long ago did that happen?"

"Two years."

Will scribbled that down. Why would the woman wait two years for revenge? That was Will's next question. While they discussed that, I stood and wandered over to a glass side table. A row of photos in black-bordered frames sat on it. One of the photos showed Mr and Mrs Fairchild with two sour-faced teenagers—a boy and a girl. I jumped into a break in conversation. "Are these your kids?" I turned the picture towards Mr Fairchild.

His expression fell into disgust. "No. They're Addie's kids from her first marriage. They stay here every second week. A couple of brats, they are. So spoiled. Their father has no idea what discipline is, and as much as I love Addie, she gave them whatever they wanted. I think she felt guilty because she'd divorced their father after he had an affair."

"Oh, okay." What else could I say? Will and I shared a look. If I could bet on it, I'd bet we were going to pay them a visit sooner rather than later. Although, James was probably already planning on speaking to the ex.

"Did her ex-husband have any beef with her?"

He barked out a sarcastic laugh. "I doubt it. They hardly spoke, but she was the one with the money. He did rather nicely out of the divorce. He should be thanking her, if you ask me."

A woman strode through the door and stopped short. "Oh, sorry to interrupt." She looked to be in her late twenties. Slim, long blonde hair, big fake lips and boobs, small waist, and wearing a tight-fitting red dress. Her wide eyes took in Will and me, then shot to Mr Fairchild.

He cleared his throat. "This is Heidi, our domestic assistant." Domestic assistant? Was that a high-end name for their… maid? Also, unless it was her afternoon off, she had interesting work clothes. I begged my eyebrows to stay where they were. A prematurely judgemental jump wouldn't look professional.

"I just wanted to let you know that I've made your dinner. It's on the stove. There are instructions for heating it up. I'm off now." She looked at Will and me. "Have a good evening." For someone who was leaving, she didn't have a handbag or keys. Interesting.

"Bye, Heidi." Mr Fairchild watched her with a sad face as she left the room. Will looked at me, and I raised one brow.

Will poised his pen. "How long has she worked for you?"

"Almost two years."

"I noticed she's not a witch. Does she know about you?"

"Yes. She used to date a witch, and she's *sworn* to stay silent." Ah, one of those spells. I supposed that made her not a suspect since Mrs Fairchild was killed with magic and at her office. His brow furrowed. "You don't need to interview her, do you?"

"At this stage, no." Will's eyes narrowed ever so slightly. "You aren't having an affair with her, are you?"

Mr Fairchild's eyes widened. "No, of course not! I would never cheat on Addie. She was everything to me." He stood. "I'm afraid I'm rather upset about this whole thing. I don't want to answer any more questions."

"Can I look at your phone?" Will stood. "I'll need to check it for the caller's number."

"The number didn't show up."

I stood and put up my hand. Angelica had me well trained. "Excuse me, but can I use your bathroom?"

Mr Fairchild waved his arm towards the door and hallway beyond. "There's a bathroom out there. Third door to your left."

"Okay, thanks." I smiled and hurried out. Rather than going to the bathroom, I went through the foyer and along the hallway until I was hidden from the living room. I didn't draw from the river but rather my own reserves to keep it "quiet." I slid my phone out of my pocket and pointed it at the foyer. "Show me Mr Fairchild kissing Heidi goodbye in the last month."

You know when you hope things aren't what they seem and that people will surprise you in a positive way? Well, I wasn't surprised. I clicked off a shot of Mr Fairchild and Heidi with their mouths mashed together, and he had a handful of her backside. So disappointing. Why were people so predictable? Squirrels were predictable in an entirely different way—they were skittish and cute as all get out. No wonder I loved them more than most people.

"Show me Mr and Mrs Fairchild fighting in the last week." The view through my phone stayed the same. Maybe he was telling the truth about them getting along. Maybe she didn't know about the bit on the side. "Show me Mr and Mrs

Fairchild fighting in the last month." Things changed. The glass panels above the oversized double front doors turned black, and the foyer chandelier sparkled in all its crystal glory. I snapped a shot of Mrs Fairchild with her arms folded and her face twisted in anger and Mr Fairchild with his hands gripping her upper arms. A pleading expression stained his face.

Will's voice came loudly from the living room but close to the doorway to the foyer. "Okay, well, we'll check out your phone records and see if we can't trace where this came from." He was speaking louder than normal, obviously figuring I'd gone to do some sleuthing. "We'll do a quick sweep of outside before we go."

I put my phone back in my pocket and strode into the foyer as Will and Mr Fairchild stepped into it. I gave Will a tiny nod so he knew I'd found something. "Are we leaving?" I asked, all innocence.

"Yes." Will turned to Mr Fairchild and held out his hand to shake.

They shook. "Thank you, Agent Blakesley. Please let me know what you find out. The sooner you catch my wife's killer, the better."

"I will. And for the time being, I'd limit the places you visit and employ some kind of security, at least for your house."

He nodded. "Yes. We have a security firm we deal with for the office and events. I have them coming over tonight to plan what I'll need."

"Good." Will turned to me. "We're going outside to make sure no one's lurking. Then we'll go back to headquarters."

"Okay."

Mr Fairchild opened the front door, and I stepped out onto a mosaic-tiled front verandah. Four steps down took me to a path through the front garden, which snaked through hedges and a few mature trees to the high brick front fence in the distance. I shouldn't have been surprised that the land was huge. The front door clunked shut. Will joined me on the path. He made a bubble of silence. "Take those pictures. Then we're out of here."

I glanced around. I couldn't see the neighbour to one side, but I did see a roof on the other. "Is it safe to just make a doorway?"

Will surveyed our surrounds. "Yep. This is pretty private. That's what money buys you."

"Seems like it also buys you enemies, ugly furniture, and a buxom mistress."

"So, you got some photos?"

"I sure did. Okay, let's get this done." I wandered the garden and pointed my phone around. "Show me someone stalking Mr Fairchild." Didn't matter how many times I asked, nothing changed. I looked at Will. "Nothing. Either no one's stalking him, or they haven't managed to get past his security system. Hang on." I jogged towards the driveway and to the stupendous wrought-iron gates that bore the initials M & A in swirly script. It gave a clear view to the tree-lined street. I repeated my stalking question and held my phone up. "Still nothing. This supposed stalker doesn't take their job seriously. Do you think he's faking it?"

"That's always a possibility. If he got a burner phone to call himself, or got a friend to call him, we might never be able to trace who made that call." He turned and stared at the mansion. "With or without that evidence, we'll get to the bottom of this." He turned to me. "Let's get back to HQ. We'll leave from over there." He pointed to a patch of grass we'd passed before that was surrounded by tall hedges.

We walked over there and created our portals. I stepped through. Will was right behind me. "Let's see the evidence." He held out his hand for my phone. I passed it over, and he looked at the pictures. He pressed his lips together in obvious disdain at the adulterous photo.

"The first one is self-explanatory. It's within the last week. The second one was harder to get. It's not in the last week but sometime in the last month. Do you think Mrs Fairchild knew?"

"Only one way to find out. We'll have to ask him with James present." Will handed my phone back.

"Now what?"

"Well, we discounted him because James said he was being honest when he said he didn't kill her, but I'm putting him back in the pool of suspects. Maybe he was being honest because he didn't actually cast the spell." He shook his head. "We really need to be way more specific with our questions." Will pulled his phone out. "I'm going to call Ma'am. Update her before we go back."

I plonked into a chair while I waited. I could've gone out to say hello to Gus, but I didn't feel like being grossed out.

"Yes. Just at HQ…. It went okay…. Right." He paced the room, although there wasn't much space, so he looked like one of those auto-vacs hitting furniture and turning around, only to hit something else and turn. He stopped and ran a hand through his hair. "Okay. Will do. Bye." He looked down at me. "Hey, lazy bones. She needs you to do another job."

"I'm not lazy. My legs wanted a rest, and I'm not a tyrant."

He made a total bubble of silence. "We're going to the offices of the two agents to see what you can find."

I sighed. I'd done quite a bit of magicking today, and my reserves were running low; plus, I was hungry again. A chocolate muffin and coffee wouldn't have gone astray, then a nap. But it wasn't to be. I stood. "Argh, all right. What's the point though? Surely they won't be privy to any secrets that we don't already know about."

"We need more proof. When it all hits the fan, it's essential that we can back ourselves up. We're not thugs or criminals, and if we manage to get through this, we're going to have to be able to prove it." He put his phone in his pocket. "Come on. Let's get this over and done with. You're not the only one who's had enough today. Chances are that I'll have to go out again with James and interview Mrs Fairchild's kids and ex-husband."

"Sorry. I just feel like we're in a never-ending loop of work and stress."

He pulled me in for a hug. "I know, but we'll get through it, and before you know it, we'll be on a plane to Sydney."

I couldn't help but smile at that possibility. My hand found its way to his firm cheek, and I squeezed, and I wasn't talking about his face. He laughed and kissed me. When it was over, I reluctantly pulled away. "Okay, time to work. The sooner we get out of here, the better. Lead the way."

He rang the buzzer, and a couple of minutes later, Eileen, a guard who usually worked the screening on the ground floor, answered. She was masculine-looking with her shaved head and large frame, but her smile was super sweet. She unleashed it as soon as she saw Will. "Agent Blakesley. Long time, no see. How's the family?"

"Hey, Eileen. They're good, thanks. What about yours?"

"All good. Teenagers are driving me nuts, but what else is new?" She laughed heartily. I walked out behind Will. "Lily! I haven't seen you for ages either. I've been meaning to thank you for that book recommendation. That thriller you recommended really hit the spot."

"My pleasure." I smiled. "Glad you enjoyed it."

"That I did." She shut the reception-room door. "Well, I'd better get back to wandering the halls. I'll see you two later. She winked, turned, and walked away.

Will set off the opposite way. Neither of us said anything. He was probably thinking about all the work he had ahead of him, and I was wondering who the directors were supposed to answer to. Who was going to hold Angelica and the rest of us accountable for breaking some laws against witches who were trying to kill us? Was there a "higher power" we could go to for help? Or were the parliament in the directors' and crooks' pockets until something happened that they couldn't explain away?

"Here we are." Will stopped at a door and looked at it. I employed my other sight. Only one protection spell on the outer door. Will drew more magic and got to work. He was done rather quickly. "Agent Paul is good in a stoush, but his protection-spell game is lacking." Even though Will was cocky about unlocking the door so quickly, my stomach clenched. Just in case he'd missed something.

He pushed the door open. And nothing happened. I released my pent-up breath. He turned and looked down at me. "I can't believe you don't have faith in me, and after all the times I've had faith in you."

He made a good point. "Sorry. I do believe in you. It's kind of like being a back-seat driver. I can't help it. I'll do better next time. Promise." I gave him a cheesy smile, and his mouth quirked up on one corner, as if he was trying not to laugh.

We walked through the outer office. The next door had two protection spells. At least Agent Paul had tried harder with the more important door. Will narrowed his eyes. "The first one was half-arsed. These ones are way more complicated. This might take ten minutes."

There were two waiting-room chairs against one wall, and I sat in one. The receptionist desk was empty. The only thing on top of it was one of those clear plastic protection things. I wanted to ask Will why so many agents had outer offices but no secretary, but interrupting him could have deadly consequences, so I kept my mouth shut. Yay me, controlling myself for once.

My gaze roamed the room. After its tenth pass over the same table, office chair, Will, and my feet, a thought hit me. Maybe the inner office was a decoy? Maybe Agent Paul wasn't as lacking in skill as we thought. I had a quick look at the room through my phone camera for any spying bugs. None showed up. I drew magic. "Show me all the things Agent Paul is trying to hide from Angelica."

Nothing showed up immediately, so I stood and went to the receptionist desk. I opened the three drawers one by one. The top one had a couple of pens and a black diary. I picked it up and leafed through it. Empty. I put it on the table and looked through the other drawers. A few clean takeaway napkins, but that was it. Time to break out the magic. "Show me what Agent Paul doesn't want Angelica to see." I scrunched my forehead. Still nothing.

There was something, though. I knew there was. Hmm. *Think, Lily.*

I moved the chair out of the way, lay on the ground on my back, and slid my head and shoulders under the desk. When we were kids, James had a journal—he hated when I called it his diary. Being the annoying sister I was, I'd tried to find it to read it. He hid it from me in what I later found out was a secret compartment in his wardrobe. Dad had helped him make it the non-witch way. So, if Agent Paul was being sneaky, maybe the table had a hidden compartment.

I looked at the underside of the desk with my other sight. No spells. Which made sense because that would give it away. If there was something here, it was just an old-fashioned hidey-hole.

Lifting my camera, I said, "Show me any secret compartments."

A smile stretched my lips wide. "Gotcha!" *Click, click.*

There were two secret compartments, each in a different leg. It looked as if the compartments folded out and up on little arm-hinge things. I wasn't sure how to open them though, so I fumbled around, pressing the legs where the openings were in my photo. Nothing. There must be a lever or button somewhere else because there were no spells keeping them shut.

I pointed my camera at the underside of the table. "Show me someone opening the secret compartments." An arm came into shot. The person's finger pressed a small section, about an inch long, of the frame supporting the tabletop. I reached up and pressed the same spot. *Click.* Eeek, it worked! This was so exciting. I felt like a real spy for approximately two-point-three seconds.

Both secret compartment doors popped out and slid up, revealing their mysterious cavities. I reached into one and found something smooth. I pulled it out. Rolled-up paper. Now for the other cubbyhole. My fingers delved in and touched something cool and small. I hooked my pointer finger into it and scooped it out. A ring. The green glow of magic illuminated small Egyptian-style runes imprinted on the silver surface. What did this thing do? There were no identifying spell symbols in its aura. With other magical things Angelica wasn't sure about, the only way to know was to test them. Or we could ask Agent Paul. He probably wouldn't answer willingly, but I wondered if Angelica would consider compulsion. He was a double agent, after all. She was trying to keep things as aboveboard as possible, but she'd already crossed some lines. Why not cross another if it helped?

I wriggled out from under the table and stood. Sweat

popped out on Will's forehead. "Do you need some of my magic?"

"No, thanks. Almost done."

I sat down and stared at the ring in my palm. *What do you do, little ring?* There was no way of knowing right now, so I put it in my lap and unrolled the papers. There were twelve A4 sheets. They appeared to be house plans. I put the ring in my jacket pocket, knelt on the floor, and spread the papers out. Six different buildings, each with a page of floor plans and building elevations. I sucked in a breath. Crap.

"I'm done." Will turned and wiped the sweat from his brow. "What the hell?"

I stared up at him, rather proud of myself. "I found this hidden in a secret compartment in that desk. Except...." I sighed. "This doesn't look good. These house plans, from what I can tell, include Millicent and James's house and Ma'am's. They also include Beren and Olivia's place, what I think is Liv's parents' house, and two others I don't know."

Will knelt on the floor next to me and perused the plans. He swore. "You're right. These notes here, here, and here, they're outlining the various protection spells that they could decipher. They don't have them all written down, so that's something positive."

"Oh, and I forgot." I took the ring out and put it on one of the papers. "I found that as well."

His eyes widened, and he snatched it up. He turned it around, inspecting it from all angles. "Gee, Lily, you've outdone yourself today."

I smiled. "I couldn't believe how easy he made it for us to get into this room, and I figured he wanted whoever tried to break in to think that this room held nothing special compared to the other room. I mean, his inner office could still have something important in it, but I know from other times we've snooped that we don't bother much with the outer offices."

He rubbed his forehead. "You make a good point. Not a good oversight on our part." He rolled the plans up, handed them to me, and stood. "Let's see if your hypothesis is correct. Time to check out his office."

I stood and clenched my stomach muscles as Will turned the handle to the office. I knew he was good at disarming booby traps, but everyone made mistakes on occasion. The door opened without drama. Phew.

I followed him into a neat and tidy room. Agent Paul didn't have any guest seats in here. Weird, but okay. Maybe he liked to discourage visitors? His green-leather chair sat behind a glass desk. There were two sets of four-drawer metal filing cabinets in one corner against the back wall. "They both have spells locking them," said Will.

I made a bubble of absolute silence. "I'll just do a sweep of the room, then check the cabinets out."

"Okay. Thanks."

I lifted my phone up. *Show me any spying devices.* The glass table lit up, a blue glow surrounding it on my phone screen. I clicked off a shot. There were no other bugs. *Show me any video spying devices.* Nothing showed up. We were still under my absolute bubble of silence, and the table wasn't in it. "That table is a listening device, like the whole table." I showed him the picture.

He blinked. "That's a new one."

"I guess a spell would find small bugs, as would a visual on it. But who would be expecting a whole table?"

"A spell would find that, but it could be confusing because it would just show the whole table, and not with the glow, like your magic shows. I could see agents combing the table and leaving frustrated."

"Okay, so I can photograph the filing cabinets without anyone knowing. Good." I stood at the door, where I could see the whole room. *Show me whatever Agent Paul is hiding from Angelica.* The filing cabinets didn't change. My magic would likely have shown them open. I panned the phone around. When I got to the table, it showed Agent Paul sitting on his side of the table and shoving something into the steel tube that formed the legs. It was in a running-writing u shape, supporting the glass, then dipping to the floor before rising again and supporting the other side of the glass. I took a photo and showed Will.

"He's no slouch. If it weren't for your talent, he would've kept his secrets."

"Bad luck to him." I smiled. Outsmarting the criminals always sent happiness coursing through me. *Sucked in, Agent Paul.*

Will sat in Paul's chair. His magic tingled my scalp, and the silver-coloured end popped off the tube. Another roll of paper magically slid out and into Will's waiting hand. He unrolled it. After a minute, he said, "This is his contract with the directors. Got him. This is all the proof we need." He looked at me and smiled. "Ma'am is going to be pretty damn pleased with you."

"With us. You're the one who got the door open. But I agree—it was a good day's work." I yawned. "Gah, I don't feel like looking in Agent Francis's office right now. I wanna go home." I used my best whiney voice, knowing we couldn't go till we looked through her office. Whingeing about it made me feel slightly better.

"Yeah, yeah, I know. Let's just get it over and done with." He put the plug back into the tube and stood. I made my way through the office doors first and out into the hallway. Will shut the doors behind us. He drew magic and cast a spell.

"What was that for?"

"We'll be notified if someone steps over the threshold. Because the spell sits just inside, they won't see it in the door or doorframe. An alarm will sound on my phone. That's another app Millicent's dad's been working on."

"Impressive." Who said older people were slow to take on technology. From the sounds of it, he was fusing magic and tech like a champion. Yay that he was on our side. And speaking of being on our side, I wanted to go check on my squirrels. "Is there any way we can pop home and see what damage was done?"

"You know Angelica has someone on that, right?"

"But what if they don't take a good look?" Yes, I was clutching at straws. And how did they come up with that saying anyway? I didn't think I'd ever clutched a straw in my life. If you weren't careful with them, you'd squash them. Okay, so they were probably talking about the kind of straw animals ate and not the ones you drank out of, but still. Mental note: google that when I had time.

He narrowed his eyes, then gave me an ah-ha look. "You want to check on your squirrels."

"Yep. How'd you guess?" I gave him my sarcastic tone because he knew me well enough by now.

"I'm sorry, but it's too dangerous."

"How is it dangerous? They've already attacked, and they know we're not there any more. Besides, we won't be long."

He folded his arms. "Famous last words. They're probably still watching, waiting for us to make the mistake of thinking it's fine to return. And if you go looking for your squirrel army, they'll take notice. Right now, your little tree rats aren't a target, but you could change that if you're not careful."

"Grrr, they're not tree rats. Stop being mean. They're the cutest, sweetest, bravest—when they're not running away—

creatures ever, and they're my friends. I won't let you talk about them like that."

He smirked. "They're literally rodents, Lily. I didn't invent the classification. Some super-smart-scientist person did. I'm just stating facts."

I poked him in the chest with each word, but not hard. "I don't like your facts, mister." I bit my lip to keep from smiling.

He grabbed my finger. "Poke me one more time, and I'm keeping this finger." I laughed. "You think I'm kidding? There's a spell for that. We use it in interrogations all the time." His deadly serious expression had me second-guessing his threat. It wasn't out of the question. Although, I knew he'd never do that to me. But how many people had he done that to? He must've interpreted my expression because his deep rumbling laughter escaped. "I'm just kidding. You should've seen your face."

"Argh, you suck."

"Well, not totally kidding. There is a spell for that, but I've never used it."

Yikes. I was glad he'd never used it because I wasn't sure I wanted to love someone who could do that to someone else. Although, I'd done much worse, so who was I to judge? The reminder of the things I'd done lately dampened my playful mood. Worry grew through the cracks. I shook it off. We still had one more office to go through. "Come on. Let's get this done."

✿

After looking through Patty's office, which had nothing useful, we went back to Angelica's country house. Will and I sat in her study while Angelica and James poured over the evidence we'd procured. It was spread out on her desk.

Wrinkles marred James's forehead. "I can't for the life of me work out whose houses those other two are."

Angelica's poker face held a note of calmness that was unexpected. She sat back and relaxed into her chair, giving her attention to James. Had she just thrown him a meaningful look? Hmm. "I can't either." She picked up the ring from the edge of the desk. "This, however, is something I do know about, and I can't believe I'm holding it." Her gaze raked over the jewellery.

I couldn't wait all day. "So, are you going to enlighten the rest of us?"

She smiled. "Ever the impatient one, dear." The space in which I expected her to continue was jammed with silence. Her gaze stayed on mine, waiting for me to break.

I gave her what she wanted. "You're cruel. You know that?"

"Yes, dear. I'm well aware."

"Argh!"

Will smirked. "Can you please put Lily out of her misery?"

I looked at him. "Oh, so you don't want to know too?" He shrugged as if he couldn't care less. He was just as curious as me—how could he not be? He was just better at hiding it. I looked at Angelica. "Since Will and my brother don't care, maybe you could tell me secretly."

She chuckled. "Okay, dear. As you wish."

Will's eyes widened, and he jutted his chin out. "Hey, that's not fair."

"What isn't fair, dear? I thought you weren't in any hurry to find out."

He gave me a dark look, and I grinned. He shook his head. "Fine, I would like to know… please."

James watched us with a wry smile. "Okay, okay, you got me. I'd like to know too."

"This is from Egyptian times, and it's a piece that's been in witch folklore for as long as I can remember. No one has seen this—or at least no one who wanted people to know—for hundreds of years. The last recorded use of it was in 750 AD when a fellow by the name of Algernon the Usurper used it to raise an army to attempt to wipe out witches. He was a witch, of course, but his followers didn't know that. He thought if he was the only witch around, he could easily rule the middle and southwest of England, what was then known as Wessex and Mercia. A group of witches banded together to stop him, and they almost failed, but in the end, they brought him down, and after that, the ring vanished. The group hid it and made it their life's work to make sure it stayed hidden. The protection of this artefact continued through many generations of these witches, until the ring went missing again." She shook her head slowly. "And now, here it is. The question is, why does Agent Paul have it?"

"And what did he plan to do with it?" James added.

Not to be left out, Will asked, "How did he find it?"

Angelica placed the ring back on the desk. "We have quite a few questions for that man. Before we interrogate him, I think it's prudent we check his contract with the directors so we don't inadvertently kill him before we have answers." She lifted the document off the table and looked across at James. "I'm going to be a while. I want you and Imani interviewing Mrs Fairchild's children and ex-husband ASAP. If they won't speak to you tonight, I'd appreciate if you could do it tomorrow. Say whatever you must to get them to comply." She looked at Will. "I'll need you to get in touch with Millicent's father and for both of you to work out some protection spells on Olivia's parents' house. And let's not tell Olivia or Beren at this stage. There's nothing more we can do. I'd rather they were safe in their house than away somewhere we can't protect them. Can you also see if Robert knows any security witch teams we can trust? I don't like the idea of asking PIB agents to stake out the home." She pressed her lips together, a touch of anger stabbing through her calm demeanour. "The bloody directors are taking it too far, involving non-witches. This is why we have to stop them at all costs." Her façade fell away, and fear—a word I'd never normally use in relation to Angelica—emanated from her eyes. "The alternative doesn't bear thinking about." I shuddered, a vibration of warning zinging down my nape. "And, Lily, bring your mother and Olivia home. You can all have dinner together… enjoy a night off. I'll need you well rested because tomorrow could bring some… challenges." She turned her chair and stared out the window.

"Okay." There was something she wasn't telling us. I was sure of it. But what? My shoulders tightened in worry as I stood and made my doorway to grab my mum and Liv. There was no way I'd find out Angelica's secrets until she was good and ready to divulge them, which was usually at the moment everything went to hell. At least I wouldn't have to wait too long.

CHAPTER 6

The next morning started off well enough with pancakes for breakfast, but it quickly devolved into my least-favourite morning ever. Everyone else had left for work, so it was my job to feed the captives. At least the cages didn't block whoever was outside it from casting a spell to inside it. It made serving meals a whole lot safer.

Chadiot stood there with his arms folded, staring down at the bowl on his small table. His voice was whinier than I remembered. "But I hate porridge. Why do you keep serving me this tasteless rubbish? This is unacceptable." Even the other inmates stared at him with loathing.

"Oh, I'm so sorry. Would you prefer eggs and bacon, or maybe some scrumptious pancakes with maple syrup or strawberries and ice cream?"

He licked his lips, and his eyes brightened. "Can I have both?"

I smiled. "I'll see what I can do." He rubbed his hands together, and I turned and yelled towards the empty kitchen. "Can we get some eggs, bacon, and pancakes in here?" I put my hand to my ear as if I was listening. "What was that? Oh, you don't serve traitors or idiots nice food. Okay, got it." I turned to him. "Oh, I'm sorry. It seems as if the kitchen is closed for orders. Is there anything else I can get you?" Would he be stupid enough to ask for something else?

He scowled and stamped his foot. When he recovered, he said, "I suppose a cup of tea would be out of the question?"

"Ah, so you're finally catching on. Only took you a few weeks." How much torture would he endure before the universe called it even? I'd imagine at least another year. A jolt of anger pierced my chest. I hoped my squirrels were okay, not to mention Liv's parents, innocent non-witches who'd never done anything to anyone. The people in these cages had all played their part in what was happening. How could they turn on fellow agents and go against everything they supposedly stood for? I wasn't about to ask them because there was no way they'd give me an honest answer, and I didn't want them to know how much they got to me. I gave the evil eye to the other agents—because why not?—then went back to the kitchen to calm down.

I stood at the French doors and gazed out at the immaculate garden. A couple of squirrels fussed around under one of the huge trees. The need to go out and play with them broke over me like a tidal wave. I placed my hand on the glass but stayed where I was. Tempting fate was foolish. There was only a minuscule chance the directors and their cronies could trace me here, but just in case they got lucky, I didn't want to draw them to Angelica's secret home. I could take a risk at other places, but not here.

"Hey."

I jumped, and my heart raced. "Oh my God, Imani. Did you have to scare the absolute you know what out of me?"

She laughed. "Always." She came in, followed by Will.

"You're back early. What's news?"

Imani sat at the table and magicked herself a glass of water. She took a sip. "Well, looks like we have a list of suspects a mile wide. This woman was soooo popular."

Will sat next to her. "It appears that the only person who didn't hate her was her husband… supposedly."

I took a seat opposite Imani. "Recap, please." I had the feeling from my photos that she wasn't the easiest to get along with.

Will tapped the table with his pointer finger. "Let's see. Yesterday, no one said much, but they weren't exactly gushing about how nice she was. This morning, however, her ex-husband was quite open about how horrible she was, and both her kids said she was a neglectful mother—always working and too strict—and that they were happy they wouldn't have to spend time with her." Yikes, that was harsh and sad. "We managed to speak to that woman Mr Fairchild said hated her, and she did, indeed, hate her. We also spoke to a couple of their employees who had strong alibis, and they were quite open about how she was quick with the insults and spare on the praises. They were both paid extra by Mr Fairchild recently so they didn't quit."

Imani finished her water and magicked the glass away. "Oh, and we even spoke to her hairdresser. She was a demanding client and had ended up there because two other salons refused to do her hair. She'd threatened to sue one of them. Apparently, they bleached her hair two shades too light. The other salon, she abused the hairdresser and refused to pay after they did her hair because they'd made her wait five minutes before seeing her. She, of course, waited till they'd done the haircut before insulting them and walking out."

Things were starting to add up. "Wow, a lot of people had

it in for her for sure. Sounds like her crappy attitude is catching up with her. Karma, baby."

Will stared at me. "Don't sound so happy about it. Murder is never nice, Lily."

"Even when it's a disgusting human?" Was I being too harsh?

Imani looked at Will, then me, then Will again. "I'm with Lily. The world is way better off without some people in it."

"You women are ruthless."

I cocked my head to the side. "I wouldn't say that. I'd say that we're sensible realists."

"You ladies scare me."

I opened my eyes as wide as they would go. "I'm not the one who knows the remove-finger spell."

Will sighed. "Fine. You got me. But it's not like I've ever used it."

Imani raised her brow. "Oh, reeeeeeally?"

Will bit his lip. "Fine. There was just one time." He turned apologetic eyes my way. "Sorry. I didn't want you to think less of me. But Beren reattached it after the guy told us what we wanted to know. It was almost as good as new." He smiled.

"Oh. My. God. Seriously?" I sighed. I supposed sometimes things like that were justified. "Well, as long as you guys reattached it, I guess there wasn't too much harm done." Gah, now I was becoming a monster. "Just to change the subject. If everyone hates her so much, why is Angelica's acquaintance trying to get to the bottom of what happened? How is it that he wants to go to bat for her?"

"That's a very good question, love." Imani looked at Will. "What do you think?"

"Making sure the scandal doesn't go on for too long, for a start. And they're family. He knew her when she was a kid.

Maybe she didn't turn into an evil human until later? Nostalgia makes us do strange things sometimes."

I grinned. "Like paying a stupid amount for an old-looking but new fridge?"

"That's a very specific example." Will's mouth ticked up on one corner.

"It's what first came into my head. Don't ask why."

Will's phone rang. He turned to Imani. "It's Angelica." He answered it. "Hello. What's up?" He listened for a while. "Mmmhmm…. Yes…. Okay…." His eyebrows rose, surprise clear on his face. Then his eyes darkened as anger passed over him like a storm front. "Yep. Okay, leaving now. Bye." Will pushed his chair back. The screech as it skidded across the floor was brutal. He stood. What the hell did Angelica say?

Imani looked up at him. "What happened?"

"Those bastards have burnt James's house to the ground."

I sucked in a breath, and nausea rushed up my throat, choking me. "Oh my God, no!" I jumped up. "Was anyone hurt?"

Will's furious gaze found mine. "No."

Imani put her hand on his arm, maybe to calm him. "I thought you and Robert were going to beef up the protections on it."

"We didn't have time because we saw to Liv's parents' home first. Which is a good thing because they're at home. I don't think any of us would forgive ourselves if they were hurt or killed."

"But James's home. All their stuff. All of Annabelle's stuff. Her little framed baby booties, all her clothes. Millicent's wedding dress. That picture I got them for a present, of James proposing." I'd used my talent for that. Tears burned my eyes. Even though they were staying here, and the dogs and rats were safe, they were basically homeless. Millicent was going to be devastated.

"What does Angelica want us to do?" Imani asked.

"I'm to take Lily to get photos. You're coming, too, as backup. It could be a trap to entice us out there. She wants us armed and ready."

"How are we going to get there? His reception room is gone." We didn't even have a car here... or at least I didn't think we did. There was probably a garage somewhere with a vehicle in it, knowing Angelica. But how far were we from Westerham? We could be two hours' drive or more.

Will stepped away from the table so he had space. "Angelica's house is still standing, apparently. There was only minor damage outside and one of the upstairs windows was broken, but she had Lavender come by and magic it back to normal. We'll go there and grab my car."

Imani's stance was that of a gunslinger about to draw. She was totally ready for action. "But they could be waiting for us."

"My car is bulletproof, so no mucking around. Return to senders up. As soon as we leave her house, it's go, go, go. You sit in the back, Lily. I want Imani up the front with me."

"You won't get any arguments from me. You're the agents." I wasn't going to second-guess any orders. This could be a massive trap. My heart raced, and my heartbeat throbbed in my neck. I did as ordered and made my return to sender.

"If anything happens," Will said, "I'll throw a shield around us, and Imani will make a doorway to headquarters. You'll go through first, Lily." I looked at him and opened my mouth to argue, but he put extra venom in his gaze. "Don't start. This is my call."

I took a deep breath. "Sorry. I'm just hyped up and angry. How dare they burn my brother's house down!" I was almost shouting, and I'd clenched my fists, trying to contain my rage. I was so ready to let it all loose.

Abby had come into the room. She jumped up on the table. *Are you okay?*

"Yes, but no. We have a massive problem. Some evil expletive has burned James's house down." Abby hissed. "Exactly. We're off to see what we can find. You stay here and stay safe."

"Meow, brrrrrow." Which translated in my head to *okay, but you be careful too.*

"We will. Don't worry." I gave her a kiss on the top of her head. "Okay, let's do this."

We all made our doorways. I magicked the house key to myself from upstairs and went through my doorway first. At least the reception room was intact. The duck picture on the wall was straight. A good sign. I unlocked the door, opened it, and listened. Hearing nothing, I poked my head around the door. The hallway was empty. Phew.

I stepped into the hallway as Will and Imani came through their doorways. I jogged to the kitchen. Empty. I couldn't resist a look out the window to make sure there weren't any little bodies outside. The picnic table was empty. Relief. A few squirrels scampered around, and there were no dead ones. I smiled and let out a pent-up breath. *Thank the universe.* It was tempting to spell them some food, but if anyone was watching the house, they'd feel my magic, and then the squirrels would also be easy targets if they were sitting around eating.

Will's magic tingled my scalp. "Lily, come on. The longer we stay here, the more likely we'll be discovered."

I turned. He stood at the doorway. Using my other sight, I could tell he'd cast a bubble of total silence. I'd forgotten our enemies could hear us from outside. Listening spells could work at distances of fifty feet and through walls. "Sorry. I just wanted to check the squirrels."

He nodded and jerked his head towards the hallway, then turned and left. I followed him to the front door where Imani waited. She put her hand on the door handle.

"Just a moment," Will said. "I want to create an automatic lock on the door so that as soon as we shut it, we can run."

"Okay." Imani waited with one hand in place and the other holding her gun.

Will's comment had given me an idea on how to deal with the criminals hunting us, but I wasn't sure if it would work. Hopefully I wouldn't forget to mention it later because right now, I had no brain space to hold all my spells and run and get in the car while looking out for enemies, plus think about something totally different.

Will drew magic and constructed his spell. It only took a minute, and then he was saying, "Go!"

Go we did.

Imani ripped the door open and sprinted towards the Range Rover, which was close by in the driveway. She wrenched the car door open and jumped inside as the house door slammed. Eyes wide and scanning our surroundings, I grabbed the back-door handle and yanked the door open. Breathing hard, I scrambled in and pulled it shut, willing my fiancé to hurry and get in the car.

As Will opened the door, I spotted a dark-haired man peeking over the fence only twenty feet away, the glow of a deflection shield and a return to sender around him. "Will, enemy, behind you!"

He turned, gun pointed, and I opened to the power. The enemy's magic prickled my scalp. A hole appeared in the fence and a gun poked through it. Before Will had a chance to shoot, Imani fired, but the man had a shield.

Her timing, thank the universe, was perfect.

As the would-be killer dropped his shield to fire, Imani's bullet scored a direct hit, right in the middle of his forehead.

Without waiting for another criminal to jump out, Will threw himself into the car and shut his door. Within seconds, we were speeding out of the driveway. I turned in the hopes I'd catch a glimpse of the man's body—not because I was gruesome, but we needed clues and information. Who had Imani just killed?

She turned in her seat to look at me. "Don't worry, love. We'll come back later, and you can use your talent to see who he was."

I took a deep breath, trying to regulate the effects of the adrenaline dump. "Why aren't we wearing normal shields? I can't believe you forgot! You could've been killed." Anger sizzled in my stomach and pulsed into my throat with my rapid heartbeat. I was angry at the situation, not Imani and Will, but they were the only ones I could blame right now.

Will screeched the Range Rover around a corner, then briefly met my glare in the rear-view mirror, his grey eyes calm, focussed. "We wanted to draw them out. If we were shielded to the nines, they would've stayed hidden and waited for a different opportunity. This way, we have one less of them to worry about."

My eyes widened. "What the hell? Are you crazy? Also, a heads-up would've been nice." I folded my arms and jammed back into my seat. Stupid witch agents. "You've taken about ten years off my life." At this rate, if the crims didn't kill me, my loved ones would.

As we sped towards my brother's, I kept turning to look out the back window. No one appeared to be following us, but they could've called ahead to let their buddies know we were coming, assuming they figured we were headed to James's. We'd likely have a "welcoming" committee.

Imani had re-holstered her gun but kept a watchful eye out the window. "I should probably let Ma'am know what happened." She took her phone out and dialled. "Hello, Ma'am. Yes. We had an incident at your place. One deceased target. No casualties or injuries for us." She listened for a while. "Yes, of course. Will do. Bye." She spoke to Will without looking at him, her attention firmly on our surroundings. "You're not allowed to get angry, apparently."

The rear-view mirror clearly showed his deep forehead wrinkles as he frowned. "She's sending in my sister and Lavender, isn't she?"

"Yes. She said hold off on getting there for a bit. Give them a chance to arrive at their pick-up place. I'm just going to call your sister now and find out where they are."

Will slammed the steering wheel with one palm. "Damn it!"

Poor Imani shouldn't have to deal with his mini tantrum by herself. I leaned forward and put my hand on his shoulder. "We can't trust anyone else. You know that. And your sister is capable… so is Lavender. They're probably even stronger and more alert than other agents because they're invested in our safety."

He grunted and jerked the wheel to the side, flinging me against the door as he pulled over in a skid of gravel and dirt. Imani sent me a look with a raised eyebrow. I gave her a "what are ya gonna do about it" look. Imani dialled and put the phone to her ear. "Hey, love. Yes. ETA?" She nodded. "Yep. We'll come get you." She hung up and turned to Will. "Head to Anvil's Tennis Centre. It's about five minutes from James's. They'll be waiting in the parking lot."

Will glowered at Imani before checking his mirrors and

pulling out into traffic. I leaned back again. Sometimes you just needed to let them get over it themselves.

We were soon pulling into the tennis-court parking area. Sarah and Lavender stood next to a low brick building, sexy in their agent get-up. Lavender's shock of vibrant mauve hair stood out strikingly against the black of his suit. Will stopped next to them, and they jumped into the back, Lavender sliding in next to me. He grabbed my hand and squeezed before letting go. "Hey, gorgeous. Isn't this exciting!" Will rolled his eyes as he drove out of the place.

I grinned. "So great to have you two along."

Sarah leaned forward so she could wave at me past Lav. "How've you been?"

"I'm okay, but your brother's in cranky-pants mode." My smile from seeing them dissipated. "Unfortunately, they've burned James's house down."

Sarah returned my sad expression. "I heard. I'm sorry, Lily."

Will's stern big-brother voice filled the car. "Let's get this straight. No one is to do anything dangerous. We're all to be within sighting distance of each other. You want to look at something, you check with me first. Imani's my second in charge today. We give the orders. Understood?"

Lavender put a bladed hand to his forehead in salute. "Yes, sir!"

I chuckled.

Sarah's expression turned serene, and she patted Will's shoulder. "Yes, dear brother. Understood." He narrowed his eyes. Their acquiescence, if a little condescending, was probably unexpected. I was pretty sure they would obey him—they were professionals. "What?" Sarah was all innocence. "We won't do a Lily. Don't worry."

My mouth dropped open. "Do a Lily? What the…?"

Imani snorted. "Ooh, that's a good one."

"You know," Lavender said, waving his hand in a devil-may-care gesture, "say you'll listen and do as you're told, then do whatever the hell you want. It's your specialty."

I bit my lip to keep from laughing. "Sorry. I don't mean to." And I didn't. I always had exceptional reasons for going my own way. I knew Angelica and Will hated it, but that wasn't enough to always keep me in check.

Lavender patted my knee. "It's okay, darling. No one really expects you to behave all the time. We're realists, after all." Will's scowl in the mirror begged to differ.

I smiled. "Thanks. I apprec—" I sucked in a breath, and my stomach plummeted. We'd turned into my brother's street, and there it was, the smouldering mess that used to be his house. Three fire engines blocked the street, and numerous firefighters moved around doing whatever it was they did after they'd put a fire out. A couple of them stood on the grass outside the crime scene, chatting to a police officer.

Will pulled over and cut the engine. He turned around so he could address those of us in the cheap seats. "Return to senders and shields up. They likely won't try anything here with so many non-witches around, but you never know, and we have some investigating to do, and I can't keep a visual on everything. Lily, take photos straight away. Get whatever information you can. Stay with Lavender and Sarah—they can make sure you're safe. I'm going to talk to the policeman, and Imani's going to comb over the rubble." I didn't need anyone to keep me safe, surely, when I had all my spells activated, but if it made Will happy.... "Any questions?" We stayed silent, and I magicked my Nikon to myself—I needed to look official. "Okay, then. Let's go."

I slid out of the car. Smoke stench stung my nostrils. I swallowed the urge to cough. Lavender got out on my side and shadowed me to the house. Sarah soon joined us on my other side. Despite my security detail, I flicked my gaze around. There wasn't anyone suspicious here, but who was to say the crime gangs didn't have recruits in the police or fire services? Any one of the people on duty in their uniforms could be a threat. I gave them all a once-over—none seemed to be staring at us—and got to work.

Show me what started the fire. A fireball exploding out of the windows showed in my viewfinder. *Click. Show me who started it.* No one in front of the house. I turned one-eighty degrees on the spot. There, across the road. *Click.* The bearded man with the evil grin looked familiar. I couldn't be sure of it, but he looked suspiciously like one of the thugs at the warehouse we'd travelled to after escaping the leave-kill spell. Goosebumps slithered along my arms. I lowered my camera to make sure he wasn't standing there in real time.

Phew.

Show me the man from the criminal gang I'm thinking about. He appeared again. Yep, that was him.

Was anyone else helping? There to the side of the house, a woman appeared. Whether she'd assisted in casting the spell or she was adding power to it, who knew? It was enough that she was here. *Click.*

How brazen. Daylight and neither of them had cared who saw them. They'd likely worn no-notice spells. Maybe they'd also magically deactivated any video surveillance in the area. All James's surveillance cameras would be toast by now. Had they picked anything up before and sent it to his phone app? I'd have to wait to find out.

"How's it going?" Lavender asked whilst gazing behind us.

I made a bubble of total silence. "Good. I've got the two who did this. They basically blew the place up." I'd have to leave it to Imani and Will to figure out how they got past James's protective spells.

I walked closer to the house until I was just shy of the stinking, melted charcoal. Pockets of smoke rose from the middle of the debris. I scanned the remains, searching for anything salvageable. But there was nothing. I sighed, my shoulders dropping. This was going to break James's and Millicent's hearts. At least Annabelle was too young to know what had happened. And they were all safe. That was the main thing.

"Can I see?" Sarah asked. I handed her the camera and took lookout duties while she was busy. She handed the camera back. "Let's update my brother."

We made our way over to him and waited while he thanked the police officer. He turned to us. "Anything?" I handed him the camera, and he looked through the pictures. "Good work." He gave it back and glanced around. "I think we're done here. Imani should be finished in a minute. I'll go check on her. Meet me at the car."

"Okay," Lavender answered for all of us.

We sat in the car and watched the scene. Sarah shook her head. "What a disaster. There's nothing left."

I gazed out the window. "I know." I sniffed. "Argh, it still stinks." I lifted my arm up and smelled my sleeve, then grabbed my ponytail and brought it to my nose. Ew. "I need a shower."

Sarah chuckled. "Um, you're a witch. Remember?"

"Oh, yeah." I smiled at my idiocy. "How is it I can never remember?" I drew magic. "Please get rid of the stink of smoke from my hair and clothes and body." That should cover it. I sniffed my sleeve again. "All gone. Thanks for the reminder."

"Any time."

I scrunched my forehead. One of the firemen, a rangy guy, had followed Will around to one side of the rubble. My other sight told me he was a witch who was wearing a return to sender. "What's that fireman doing? The one near Will." Maybe he was an ally? I wasn't sure what damage he could do if he wasn't, considering Will had protection spells, and they were in public.

But then again, money was a great motivator, and we all had prices on our heads.

He wasn't so far away that I couldn't feel the magic when he channelled it. Alarm bells cascaded in a creepy waterfall from the top of my head, over my shoulders, and down my body. I threw the door open and bolted.

Will turned to look at the guy. The only thing he could do was tackle Will or…. I screamed out, "Hey, hey!" hoping to distract the guy. He could make a doorway and snatch Will. It was highly illegal in the circumstances—with all the non-witches around. But maybe the guy was only going to do something innocent, like make himself a cup of hot tea?

Both Will and the fireman stared at me, as did half the people on the scene. If I didn't know better, I'd say the rangy witch was giving me a dirty look. I reached them, puffing, and held out my phone to Will. I had to pretend I wasn't a crazy woman running around screaming for no reason. "The boss is on the phone." *Go along with me.*

His eyes widened ever so slightly, and he gave a nod, covering his surprise at me being in his head. It had been ages since we'd mind talked. We usually saved it for dire circumstances in case someone figured it out. "Thanks." He put it to his ear and pretended to talk while Imani approached us, and the fireman narrowed his eyes at me before turning and striding off. Grrrrr. Imani looked at me, then held her phone up and took a picture of the guy. It was only a side shot, but better than nothing. "Okay, understood. Bye." He "hung up" and gave me the phone back. He addressed Imani. "Did you get everything you needed?"

"Yes. Let's go."

Sarah and Lavender were halfway between us and the car. They turned and walked with us. Once we were all safely in the Range Rover, Will made a bubble of silence and twisted around to look at me. "What the hell was that?"

"That fireman was behind you and drawing magic. I wasn't sure what he was going to do. My money's on a doorway. The look of death he gave me when I ran over would've impressed Medusa."

Imani held up her phone. "I'll run his photo through our system."

Will got on his phone and dialled. "Hey, Liv. Can you check what fire crews are on the job at James's? Email all the names and photos. Thanks. Bye." He started the car.

"Hang on a sec!" There was one more thing I wanted to do. I hopped out and held up my phone. "Show me a witch wearing a no-notice spell." I was too far away from the guy to make out what spells he had on. Up close, I'd noticed the return to sender, but I couldn't read the other two or three spells.

Nothing happened. Had I made a judgement error? Hmm. My magic was supposed to show me what happened in the past, and I'd asked it to show me something happening now. "Show me a witch wearing a no-notice spell from ten minutes ago." Everyone had jumped places. We had just arrived and were walking towards the fire. The witch glowing in my picture was that fireman. Maybe he wasn't even a member of the fire brigade but an implant. I clicked off a shot, then got in the car. I put the photo on the screen and held the phone up so everyone could see. "See how that guy is glowing? I asked who was wearing a no-notice spell."

Imani whistled. "Wow, love. Your magic is invaluable."

"No guesses for what Liv's search will turn up." Lavender smoothed a hand over his lapel.

Yep, we needed no guesses at all.

CHAPTER 7

Will, Imani, Lavender, Sarah, Beren, and I sat in Angelica's country-house living room, waiting for Angelica, James, and Millicent. They'd moved the captives into the basement. How many more agents would we put there before this was over? Maybe Angelica could recruit and train new people and start a new PIB. Hmm, that wasn't a bad idea, if I did say so myself.

Abby had seen fit to plonk herself in my lap. I stroked her head and under her chin. There was nothing nicer than a rumbling cat's purr. It made me think of my squirrels—not that they purred, but you know—they're fluffy and cute and totally pattable. If only I could go home, round them up, and bring them here, but they wouldn't be as happy. Angelica's Westerham yard and its surrounds was their home. I just had to hope they'd all be safe until I returned.

Lavender looked at his phone. "Darlings, it's after five o'clock. It's cocktail hour! Do you think Ma'am would mind if we got into the spirit while we waited?"

One corner of Will's mouth lifted. "You never know."

I snorted, and Imani laughed. "Oh, love, I'd pay to see Ma'am's face when she walks in and sees us here with little umbrellas in our drinks."

"Well, she can't exactly fire you all. There aren't many trustworthy agents left." I wouldn't mind a cocktail—something light and fruity, maybe a mango daiquiri.

"True." Beren pretended to consider it. "With the week she's having, she might want one herself."

Angelica strode in. "Who might want what?"

We all stared at Lavender. It was his idea, after all. He smiled, his straight white teeth befitting a toothpaste commercial. If anyone could sell this idea, it was Lavender. "I was thinking a cocktail meeting is a good idea since it's technically evening. I'm rather parched, and I imagined you might appreciate one too. You're always go, go, go." He waved his hand back and forth in the air for emphasis. "You never get to have any fun. That makes me sad."

Angelica smiled, an honest-to-goodness genuine one. Wonders would never cease. "Thank you for thinking of me, but we all need to be clear-headed for this. As soon as this is over, I'll drink you all under the table. Until then, let's focus." I blinked through my surprise—I'd never seen her drunk and didn't know she was capable—as she sat in an armchair that faced our two rows of office-style low-backed chairs. We'd brought them from headquarters after checking they were bug free. We'd outgrown Angelica's study pretty quickly. Reclaiming the lounge room was fantastic. Walking in here and not seeing Chadiot had improved my mood a hundredfold.

A stony-faced James and red-eyed Millicent came in. I jumped up and ran to them. I reached around both of them and squished them in a hug. They hugged me back, and we stood that way silently for a moment. James was the first to step back. I gave them my sad face. "Are you guys all right?"

James put his arm around Millicent. "We'll be okay. At least no one was hurt."

Millicent sniffled. "James is right, but, yes, I'm devastated." She blinked back tears.

Anger flared within me. "We'll get everyone who did this. I'll zap them all a new one. I haven't killed anyone for a while."

James raised his eyebrows. "You killed someone not even two weeks ago. You're kind of scaring me right now."

I laughed, but not in a crazy way. I wasn't quite there yet. "I'm scaring myself too, but they're evil. The world is better off without them."

"Hear, hear." Good old Imani always had my back.

James employed his patient parent voice. "Still, we'll arrest them and throw them in jail for life. Killing them is making it too easy—they won't have time to suffer and consider what they've done. Besides, I don't like the thought of you wanting to kill people. You've always had a good heart, and I know you feel guilty, even if we all know sometimes there's no other option. But in this case, there is another option."

Typical James, bringing me back to reality and caring about my soul. Millicent gave me a sad smile. "Thanks for the sentiment, though, Lily. To be honest, I'd like to kill them myself." James gave her a "let's not do that" look. She shrugged.

Angelica cleared her throat. "If we could get started, please, we have a lot to cover."

I gave them one last hug and went back to my chair. James and Millicent took their seats behind me. James's magic tingled my scalp, and a white backdrop appeared on the wall behind and to Angelica's right. He was back in agent mode. "Lily."

James tapped my shoulder. "Can you pass me your phone? We'll quickly look through all your photos before we start."

"Yeah, sure." I unlocked it and handed it to him. I'd transferred all the pictures from my Nikon to my phone so I could email them to Angelica.

"Which ones do you want to start with?" he asked Angelica.

Irritation or frustration, I wasn't sure which, flashed in her gaze. She quickly banished it and threw up her poker face. "The murder investigation. As much as I want to put those goons out of action, Phillip rings me every couple of hours asking for information. I'd like to be able to tell him that we've solved the case." Wow, he needed her help, not the other way around. Maybe he should learn some patience. Yes, he was bereaved, but how quickly did he think murder cases were solved when half the people the victim came into contact with wanted them dead?

James did whatever it was he did, and the first photo I'd taken of Mrs Fairchild's body appeared on the screen. Angelica turned her seat side-on to us so she could see it. "According to Agent Floyd, the entry wounds indicate the lightning strike came from a slight angle above." The picture changed to the conference room. "But, as you can see, there isn't any evidence of it coming through the ceiling. Lily and I went to the floor above, but we couldn't find evidence of anyone casting a spell from there." The picture changed to show the silvery residue. "Agent Floyd is still analysing the substance. He should have an answer for me this afternoon." The picture of Mr Fairchild and his girlfriend was next.

"Nice get, Lily."

"Thanks, bro." It was nice to get praise from James. "Are we ruling her out because she's not a witch?"

"I'm not sure." Angelica folded her arms. "So far, the

evidence says it was a witch, but I'm not ready to discount her yet. If it was the husband, she could've helped."

"But he was telling the truth when he said he didn't kill her." Frustration peppered James's tone.

"Yes, Agent Bianchi, but he could've paid someone else to do it and technically been telling the truth—he didn't do it with magic. Talents can be a little too word sensitive sometimes. And we know that it is possible for people to fool that particular talent if the person speaking believes what they're saying enough." I found it hard to believe that James wouldn't pick up a lie. He'd never failed to catch me out when we were growing up, even before his proper magic came in. Talents could manifest early if the witch didn't need power from the river to create them.

The next two photos to come up were the ones I'd taken of Mrs Fairchild getting upset at the accountant lady and checking the other person's computer. "Upon further questioning, Marian admitted Mrs Fairchild was constantly checking over her work and insisted on viewing a final file to okay before sending it herself to the board of directors. I had the feeling there were other things she wasn't telling us, but I wasn't able to get anything else out of her."

I leaned forward. "*You* interviewed her?"

"Yes, dear. I do that from time to time. We're understaffed, especially when you take out the agents I can't trust, and it's essential that this case is handled impeccably." I didn't miss the concerned look she shot at James. It was only a second, but I'd gotten to know her well, add to that me studying her poker faces for any hint of emotion, and I was ready to catch those snowflakes when they fell.

"Agent Roche is more than ready to offer assistance." Sarah gave Angelica a meaningful look. "We're just waiting for you to ask. The last few weeks, Agent Roche, Lav, and I have been looking carefully at all our agents. Roche told a couple of them—close friends—your dilemma, and they subjected themselves to an interview after swearing to tell the truth or die. So, that's two more agents you can definitely trust." The head of the French PIB, Agent Roche, had come through for us more than once. He was one of the good ones.

She raised her chin a smidge. "He's jumped the gun. We'll manage. At least he knows which of his staff he can truly trust." We all had our faults, and I suspected that Angelica's was her pride. She couldn't deny that she needed the help, and it wasn't as if it were personal. This was for the good of the PIB and British people.

Will's leg bumped mine. Abby—who'd been jolted—and I looked at him with what-the-hell faces. *It's not that. She doesn't want to make anyone else a target.*

Oh. Sorry. I should've known. I checked my mind shield was up. Yep. He just knew my facial expressions too well. Poker face, where are you when I need you? I blanked my face as best I could. The last thing Angelica needed were judgey Lily faces right now.

Beren put up his hand, and Angelica gave him a nod. "Have you got any hypotheses as to how someone out of the room could've cast the spell that killed Mrs Fairchild?"

"I'm glad you asked, dear. We have a few options. One is that the killer managed to put a freeze spell on the two witches who were in the room and then mind wipe them. Two is that those in the room helped and somehow managed to get past Agent Bianchi's almost-infallible talent. Three is that an incredibly powerful witch found a way to suspend that spell in mid-air, invisible to everyone's other sight, and time it to perfection." She folded her hands in her lap. "So, team, which of the three do you think happened?" Everyone looked at each other. Imani was the first one brave enough to raise a hand. "Yes, Agent Jawara."

"They're all long shots. And surely Lily would have found something with her camera in that room if they'd been in there."

"Good answer. You're at the stage I'm at. And it's a damn frustrating one."

Beren rubbed his forehead. "This is doing my head in. We're going around in circles."

Angelica's phone rang. She looked at it. "I have to take this." She held it to her ear. "Hello. What do you have for me?" She made some positive noises as she listened. Hopefully it was Agent Floyd with some good news. The sooner we got this case done, the sooner we could go after the directors. As nice as this country house was, Angelica's Westerham house felt like home. There was also the little matter of me having a price on my head. The sooner it was gone, the better—the bounty, not my head, obviously.

She hung up, and James asked, "Do we have good news?"

Angelica twisted her mouth to one side. "That depends on what you think qualifies news as good. It's not bad, but it hasn't blown the case wide open, unfortunately. The powdery substance around the wounds is paint, pulverised to near dust with the heat of the lightning spell. Crème brûlée interior matt paint, to be exact."

Will scratched his thigh. "It won't take long to find out what paint is on the walls in that room."

"No, it won't. Can you call Mr Fairchild and find out when it was last painted, etcetera?"

"Will do." Will stood and went into the hallway.

"If it is paint from that room, what does it mean?" I couldn't, for the life of me, work it out.

"I'm not sure either, believe it or not." Her tone was serious, but she gave me a slight smile. "Actually, you didn't take a photo of the moment she was struck. We'll need one."

"Oh, crap. Sorry. I was too intent on asking who killed her because I figured we knew how she died. It should've covered everything, but it was just black."

Angelica looked at James. "Can you take her back there right now? I hate to admit it, but we're floundering for answers, and I don't want to sit here wasting time discussing things without as many facts as we can get. We'll stay here and try and come up with a plan for the directors while you're gone. It should only take you ten minutes, tops."

James and I stood. He gave a nod, and we went to the other end of the room, where he made a doorway to the Fairchild offices. He gestured at me to go first. I magicked my camera to myself before we stepped through. The receptionist answered the door when we buzzed. Because she wasn't expecting us, she called Mr Fairchild. He gave us the okay, which made me think he either didn't do it or he "knew" we wouldn't find anything. Lucky my talent was a secret. If news got out, being a target wasn't the only bad thing—crims would wise up and plan better. The criminals who wore face coverings when offending were way ahead of the others without even realising it.

Back at the conference room, I stood at the door. James kept a lookout so no one could observe me too closely. I took a photo of where she'd stood for reference; then I called on my magic. *Show me the moment Mrs Fairchild was killed.* Sure enough, Mrs Fairchild appeared. She stood facing the conference-room table where her two employees sat looking up at her. A bright flash led from the ceiling to her head. The lightning hadn't yet arced all the way to her chest. Her companions had their arms halfway to their faces. I asked for the next moment so I had a catalogue of how it happened. As the brightness reached her chest, the other two had their arms in front of their eyes. The beat after that and Mrs Fairchild had staggered back a step, already falling. *Click*.

I lowered my camera. It was time to show my findings to Angelica.

❧

Back in her lounge room, we'd just scrolled through the pictures. She returned it to the second one I'd taken. "Right, so we can all but rule out those two for murder. There was no evidence that they planted any spells beforehand, and at that moment, they're busy protecting themselves." She looked at James. "Can you cross them off our list? We need to narrow this down, and based on all the evidence and their interviews, I'm ready to start making hard decisions."

James magicked an iPad to himself. "Consider it done."

Angelica stood and put her hands on her hips while staring at the screen. "It doesn't seem to be coming from the ceiling, but the vicinity of the ceiling. It's a shame it's too bright to see what's actually going on." Rather than specific detail, it was just an explosion of light, the middle a more opaque line that reached for the victim.

"So where did the paint come from?" I just didn't get how paint residue got in there.

Angelica shook her head. "Maybe the spell scraped the ceiling before it descended?" She brought the reference photo up. "But there's no evidence of blackening anywhere." She blew out a loud breath.

James's phone rang. "Hello, Agent Bianchi speaking…. Oh, really. Thank you so much. No, no, I'll come to you. What's your address?" He wrote it on the iPad. "See you shortly." He hung up. "That was a witch hairdresser from the last place Mrs Fairchild was banned from. She wants to talk to us."

"Okay. Why haven't we already interviewed her?"

Imani answered, "We spoke to the owner who'd banned Mrs Fairchild, and the eighteen-year-old who'd done her hair. They both said they were the only ones working when she came in, which is why they were slightly late serving her. I checked their booking diary, and there were no other hairdressers rostered on that day. The other two staff in the salon when we were there didn't say anything to dispute that."

Angelica turned to James. "Take Lily with you. If this other hairdresser has a different account, pay a visit to the hairdressing salon, and be discreet."

"Yes, Ma'am," we both answered. How was it that I was doing so much work? Was it a lie I told myself that I wasn't an agent? I might as well be one for all the investigations I was assisting in.

Again, we went to the other side of the room, and James made a doorway. "The lady's name is Brooke Chandler."

I stepped through and rang the bell, James coming through straight after me. A short, slim lady in her forties answered the door; her shoulder-length straight hair gave Lavender's a run for his money. It was vivid blue and matched her eyes. "You must be the agents."

I smiled. "Yes. I'm Lily, and this is Agent Bianchi."

"Pleased to meet you. I'm Brooke. Please come in." She stood aside. "The first door on the left is the living room. Just go in and take a seat."

When we were all seated, James started. "You said you had something you had to tell us."

She leaned forward, elbows on her thighs, and wrung her hands. "This has to stay confidential. I don't want to lose my job."

James's brows drew down. "If your employer broke the law, we're going to have to go after her. I'm sorry, but that's just how it is."

"I know, but if you could try and make out like you figured it out for yourselves, I would really appreciate it."

I didn't know why no one else thought of it, but I had to say it. "If your employer goes to jail, you maybe won't have a job anyway. So you have nothing more to lose." Hmm, that didn't quite come out how I wanted it to.

Brooke sighed. "I know, but if the clients don't find out I had something to do with it, I can start my own salon and take them with me." She blushed. Meh, who could blame her for wanting to keep getting paid work?

James used a soothing tone. "Don't worry. We'll be discreet."

She bit her lip, then took a deep breath. "Okay, so I overheard Cynthia telling those other agents that Mrs Fairchild was horrible and rude because they left her waiting five minutes before her appointment. That's not what went down at all. Rose, Cynthia's daughter, was the hairdresser who cut her hair, and she did a terrible job of it. She even snicked Mrs Fairchild's ear in the process, which bled on her white shirt, but even then, Mrs Fairchild didn't say too much. I mean, she did say ouch and told her to be careful, but wouldn't anyone?"

I nodded. "Totally." James looked at me, his lips pressed together, his expression aggravated. Okay, so we needed to be professional, but this story was getting good. So what if I was invested in it? I looked at Brooke. "Sorry. Go on."

She smiled. Yay! She understood. James could go jump. "Well, when Cynthia saw what happened, she was worried. She told me later she didn't want Mrs Fairchild to sue us—we all knew how rich she was. She's well-known in our area. It was a coup that she changed salons and came to us."

I frowned. "If that's true, why did Cynthia let her inexperienced daughter cut her hair?"

She rolled her eyes. "Exactly. Cynthia's actually a great hairdresser. I could've done it, or so could've Fatima, but Cynthia's daughter pushed her mother into it when she saw the booking. She cried and threatened to quit and tell her father what happened. Rose thinks she's a, and I quote, 'Great *artiste.*'"

I stared at Brooke in shock. "Oh my God. What a brat. Are you sure she's not twelve?"

Brooke laughed. "I know, right?"

James gave me another one of his "looks," but I ignored it. "So then what happened?" This was better than *Days of Our Lives.*

"Well, she stuffed up, and they're not witches. I have no idea why Mrs Fairchild would've risked it. Anyway, Cynthia decided to strike first, and after Mrs Fairchild left, she made up a story that she was a difficult client—not hard when people tend to believe the worst of people, especially if they're rich and well-known. She also told people that she'd banned Mrs Fairchild from the salon, which also wasn't true."

"Why didn't Mrs Fairchild say anything or threaten to sue for defamation?" Maybe she was a difficult person and didn't want to dredge up trouble? Or maybe she didn't even care?

"I don't know. I've heard from others that she can be demanding and cranky, so maybe she thought she wouldn't win? All I know is that after that happened, she never came back, but while I was working next to them, my client asked me how things were, and I was honest and told her that I was having trouble paying rent while I looked for another house-mate. My best friend finally moved in with her fiancé, but in the interim, it left me way short each month. Mrs Fairchild joined the conversation, and before I knew it, she'd asked for my bank details, and that evening, she gifted me five-hundred pounds. I wouldn't normally let someone do that, but I was on the verge of being evicted. You see why I couldn't let their lie stand… at least not with you guys. No matter what anyone else has to say about her, she was a generous, kind woman."

That was unexpected.

"Can provide us proof of that payment?" James would know she was telling the truth, but we needed a paper trail.

"Of course. I'll email it to you."

"Thanks. Was there anything else?"

"When I called her office to thank her, she also provided a few phone numbers to charities that could potentially help me till I got someone else in. She really went above and beyond." She grabbed a chunk of blue hair and gave it a small tug. "That's it. That's all I can tell you."

"Thank you, Miss Chandler. I'll make sure this stays secret from your boss." James stood and looked down at me. "Come on. You can use my doorway."

I was pretty sure that was code for "We're going to a toilet near the hair salon." I stood and smiled at Brooke. "Thanks for coming forward. I'm sure Mrs Fairchild would appreciate it if she knew."

She shrugged and stood. "Right is right, you know?"

"I do." And that was why we had to fight with everything we had to ensure the PIB wasn't destroyed, or there'd never be any justice for people like Mrs Fairchild and thousands like her. When I stepped through James's doorway, my resolve was stronger than ever.

CHAPTER 8

After taking photos at the salon, we returned to Angelica's. Unfortunately, Will, Beren, and Imani had to leave and deal with another case they were close to finishing. Lavender and Sarah had gone back to Paris, so only Angelica and Millicent remained.

"Don't worry, dear," Angelica was saying to Millicent as they stood together, "you can stay here as long as you like." They turned and looked at us as we walked in. "What do you have for me?" I knew she was asking James, so I stayed quiet. See, miracles did happen.

James updated her on everything, and then I handed her my camera. I'd taken two photos at the salon from outside, since the shopfront was glass. I was able to get all five client seats in the shot, which proved that Cynthia had lied about who was in that day. I also managed to use my zoom lens to get a good picture of the cut ear. I was just lucky it had been the one facing me. So Brooke's account checked out.

James brought up his email on the iPad. "Here's the proof of the five-hundred-pound deposit as well."

Angelica handed the iPad back. "So neither of these ladies could've done it because they're non-witches. *But* we have proof that maybe Mrs Fairchild isn't as bad as what some others have said."

"That about sums it up." Okay, so it was unnatural for me to not talk out loud for more than five minutes at a time, unless, of course, I was talking to myself in my own head. "So now what? Do we have a shortlist of who might have done it?"

Angelica looked at James. He opened a file on his iPad. "The ex-husband and husband are both on our list. The current husband and kids were in her will, apparently, and each of them stood to inherit tens of millions. The ex-husband has had money issues lately, so he'd benefit from the children making bank, and the current husband brought substantially less money to the relationship than she did. We're also still considering the accountant Lily took a photo of. More than one of her work colleagues told us there was no love lost between her and Mrs Fairchild. Mrs Fairchild had threatened to fire her before, apparently. We were supposed to speak to her today, but she's called in sick to work. Do you want us to visit her home?"

Angelica scratched her chin. "Call her. See if she'll talk to you today. Who else is on the list?"

"There was another employee she'd given a warning to about a month ago. When we spoke to him, he said he didn't kill her, but he admitted he hated her. Said she'd treated him so badly that he was looking for another job before she was killed. He wouldn't let us check his computer though, and unless we have a stronger reason, we're not going to get a look at it."

"But he checked out with your talent?"

"Yes."

I sat down because standing sapped more energy than walking. How did that even work? "So, either someone's lying, or we haven't spoken to the killer yet. And even though the housekeeper was likely shagging the husband, she's a non-witch so couldn't have done it."

"Yes, dear. There is something we haven't looked into: Did they have any disgruntled clients? They manage people's money. Have they lost a lot of it lately?" Angelica's question was met with three blank stares. "Right." She turned to Millicent. "Can you speak to Mr Fairchild and ask for those details? He might be reluctant to drag clients into this, but we need to know." She looked at James. "Whatever you need to do to speak to the accountant today, do it. She'll also know whether they've lost client money, and I have a feeling she'll be more willing than Mr Fairchild to talk about it. You can also ask her about her relationship with the deceased."

"On it." James magicked his iPad away and pulled his phone out of his pocket. He called the Fairchilds' office. Luckily the receptionist was compliant, and he didn't have to threaten anyone with a court order. The real test would come when he called the accountant. If she didn't want to talk, we would have to take her to the PIB for questioning, and she could refuse to talk. I hoped that wasn't what was about to happen.

While James called Marian Arthur, Millicent made her doorway and departed. Angelica looked at me. "I have to leave. Make sure you update me as soon as you have some answers."

I nodded. "Will do, Ma'am."

"Thank you. Goodbye, dear." James gave her a nod as she made her doorway and exited.

After a couple of minutes of redialling the number and

leaving one voice message, James gave up. "She's not answering. The receptionist gave me her address. Let's just go. What's the worst that can happen?"

"She has a reception room full of poisonous spiders?" I tried not to smile.

He gave me an uber unimpressed look. "Very funny. Come on." He made a doorway, and off we went.

Thankfully her reception room didn't have any spiders. It was rather elegant, in fact. French-style furniture decorated the room—two single chairs and a side table with a pretty blue-and-white vase. There were even yellow tulips in it. Were they real? I leaned over and felt a petal. Yep, real.

"What are you doing? Stop touching things."

"I wanted to know if they were real or fake. You can tell a lot about a person from their flowers."

He narrowed his eyes. "Like what?"

"Like, whether they like real or fake flowers." I grinned. "Ha, I have no idea. I just thought it sounded good."

"I swear to God, Lily, sometimes…."

The door handle made a noise, and the door opened. I recognised the middle-aged woman. Marian Arthur. Looked like we might get lucky. Although, the suspicious look on her face might mean otherwise. "Who are you, and what are you doing at my door?"

James introduced us and produced his badge. "I'm Agent Bianchi from the PIB, and this is my assistant, Lily. We're investigating the murder of Mrs Fairchild, and we had some questions about client finances. Would you mind talking to us? It shouldn't take too long. I tried calling, but you weren't answering, and this matter is urgent, so we were hoping you could spare some time today."

She regarded us for a long, long moment, her face stony.

I smiled. "I love your tulips. They're so happy." James widened his eyes at me. The message was clear—shut up!

She blinked, as if surprised by my random comment. Her expression broke, and she smiled. "Why thank you. I have them delivered once a week—one bunch for the reception room, one for my bedroom, and a lovely large bunch for my family room. I find they make the house warmer and cheerier."

"I'd have to agree with you. The yellow goes so well against the blue in here too."

Her chest rose with a large breath. "Thank you. And we might as well get this over and done with. Please come in."

If she hadn't been watching us come in, I would've poked my tongue out at James in a "so there" statement. My gut told me to just say what I was thinking, and I was right. I did allow myself a small, self-satisfied smile. It would have to do for now. I could rub James's nose in it later.

We stopped in the foyer while Marian shut the door. "Please, follow me." She took us along a wide, tiled corridor to a doorway that led to a massive kitchen that opened to a conservatory-style dining and living area.

I sucked in a breath. "This is stunning." The island alone had six dark timber seats at it, which contrasted well against the white-marble waterfall benchtop. Was the six-burner gas stove and double oven for show since she was a witch?

She must've seen my expression—because I had no filter, even for my face. Gah. "I love cooking the non-witch way. I find it relaxing." She pointed to a wicker lounge with a colourful rainforest-and-parrot fabric. "Please sit. Can I get anyone some tea?"

James, who'd donned his poker face, declined for both of us. "We just had some at the office, but thanks anyway."

"Can I interest you in some lemon muffins?" A tray with said muffins appeared in her hands.

My mouth dropped open. "Yes, please!"

"No, thank you." James gave a minute shake of his head at me.

I took a muffin off the plate and sniffed it. "Oh, this smells so good." She smiled. Then something unexpected happened. A squirrel with only half a tail scrambled up the couch and sat next to me. Oh my God, she had a pet squirrel! The more I knew about this lady, the more I liked her.

The squirrel stared at me, the muffin, then me again. *Want.*

I looked at Marian. "Can your squirrel have some?"

She gave an affectionate look at the animal. "That's Halfie. She lost her tail in a dog attack a year ago. I saved her, and she lives with me now. She has a little squirrel door to go in and out as she pleases, but she chooses to stay here. I don't like her eating unhealthy food, but you can give her a tiny bit."

I grinned. "Thanks!" I broke off the smallest bit and put it on the floor. "Here you go, Halfie."

She scurried down, grabbed it, and looked up at me. "Chitter, chitter." *Thank you.*

"You're welcome."

Marian sat and put the plate on a side table. She addressed James. "So, what would you like to know?" Her accommodating and relaxed expression was a far cry from the woman who opened the door. I'd like to think my friendliness—and probably oddness—warmed her up. Also, she didn't look sick at all. What was the real reason she'd avoided work today?

"Do you know of any serious client complaints in the last twelve months?"

"Do I need a solicitor?"

"I don't know. Have you done anything illegal?" James kept his tone calm and pleasant.

She sat up straighter and lifted her chin. "No. Definitely not. That's what I love about accounting—it's black and white. The figures add up or they don't. I deal in numerical facts and tax laws. If I ever see a discrepancy I can't explain, I speak...." Her shoulders sagged. "I *spoke* to Mrs Fairchild."

"So, has the company had any complaints that might lead to murder?"

"There were two cases. The clients threatened to sue for negligence, but those cases didn't go ahead as far as I know. At least not yet anyway."

"What kind of negligence? How much money are we talking about?" James made notes as the conversation progressed.

"The first one was around two-million pounds."

I gasped. "The company lost that much money for just one person?"

"Unfortunately, yes. Mr Fairchild handles the big money, and sometimes it doesn't go as planned. But for many of our larger clients, that's small change to them. In any case, the client wasn't impressed. He took out his other six million pounds and gave it to another company."

James stopped writing and looked at her. "I'll need that client name and their contact details when we're done, please."

"Of course." She took a deep breath. "The other one wasn't as big a loss, but it was a smaller investor. It was all the money they had. Mrs O'Connor gave us her retirement fund to manage. One point one million pounds, give or take a few thousand. Mr Fairchild lost her money, and Mr Reed's, because he put it into a medical company that recently floated. They had potentially ground-breaking cancer diagnostics, but after three years, they fell at the last hurdle. The company ran out of money to modify and further test their product and went bust."

"I'll need the name of that company as well."

"Hang on a moment." Her magic prickled my scalp. Soft magic—not too powerful—and kind. It made me think she was likely being honest with us. Based on how her magic felt, I couldn't believe she'd killed Mrs Fairchild. But what did I know?

Her laptop appeared on her lap. She opened it and tapped on the keys. Finally, she said, "Ecronivase. They have a PO box."

"And have you ever spoken to either of these disgruntled clients?"

She looked thoughtful. "No. I didn't deal with those matters. When something untoward happened, Mr Fairchild liked to handle things himself. His philosophy is that the buck stops with him, and he wanted the clients to know that their concerns were being heard."

James cocked his head to one side. "Did they pay any money back to them, out of the company's reserves?"

She magicked her laptop away and sagged back into her chair. "Mr Fairchild said they should, but Mrs Fairchild was reluctant. She called a meeting with me a few months ago and asked to look through all the books. She wanted to know if the company could afford such big payouts. We have cash, but most of the company's money is tied up in bonds, property, shares. There's an emergency fund, but that would've cleaned it out."

I remembered the photo I took of Marian and Mrs Fairchild arguing. I cleared my throat. I wasn't supposed to be asking questions, but I needed to know. "Is there anything you and she disagreed about?"

Her eyes widened slightly. Maybe she was wondering how I managed to get it right. She swallowed. "Um, well." She blew out a big breath and looked at the ceiling. "I'll lose my job for this if Mr Fairchild finds out." James and I kept our mouths shut. It wasn't as if we could guarantee anything. If she kept going, she kept going. "Oh, stuff it. Mrs Fairchild wasn't my favourite person, but she deserves justice. If I can help in any way, I want to. Right, so, she wanted to refuse payment, and I'd been ordered by Mr Fairchild to okay the payments. We had a huge argument, and she said if I didn't hand over all the paperwork for those transactions, she'd put me on probation. I was mortified. That was one step short of getting fired, and I'd been with that company since they started. The pay is actually very good, and when Mrs Fairchild wasn't on the warpath, it was a pleasant place to work." She shook her head. "I weighed up my options as to who would fire me if I went against them, and Mrs Fairchild won hands down. So I gave her everything she was asking for. I didn't hear anything about it after that."

"Did they pay?"

"Not that I know of. Mrs Fairchild is wealthy in her own right." Halfie scooted up the chair and to Marian's chest, where she snuggled into the crook under her chin. Marian stroked her little body. "I don't know if she did off the books. A scandal like that getting out would decimate their good reputation, and if they paid out from the company, it would look like an admission of guilt rather than the fickleness of markets and company fortunes. Mrs Fairchild didn't say as much, but I think she was worried about their reputation, even if the company paid without admitting fault."

"I'm sorry I have to ask you this, but did you kill Mrs Fairchild?" James didn't drop his poker face. Whether he thought she did or didn't was a mystery. It made sense that the questions were put to her in a neutral way. It wasn't like she was under arrest, and if her guard was down in this environment, all the better.

"No. Most definitely not."

James gave a small nod. "Do you know who did?"

"No. I wish I could tell you, but I have no idea. There were a few people at the office who didn't like her—she was tough but mostly fair, but when she was tough, you never forgot it. But I don't think anyone hated her enough to kill her."

"Do you think Mr Fairchild did it?"

She shook her head. "No. He was loving towards her at the office. They had the occasional argument, but never anything too bad. She spoke of him quite highly as well. Everything seemed relatively good between them." She reached over and broke off another small piece of muffin for Halfie and fed it to her.

James stood. "Well, thank you so much for speaking to us today, Ms Arthur. You've been very helpful, and we appreciate it. I did want to ask—off the record—why you called in sick today?"

She gave us a sad smile. "I lost my mother and younger sister to cancer last year. The whole thing is triggering for me, and I needed a day to adjust. As much as Mrs Fairchild and I weren't best friends, I did respect her. She was generous and gave money to various charities, and she fostered professionalism within the office. It had the most equal playing field I've experienced. Jobs were given on merit—not because of what someone had under their clothes or who their family was." She stood. "If I can be of any more assistance, let me know; just don't come to the office."

I stood as James reached out and shook her hand. "We promise not to do that."

"Thank you."

I smiled. "It was lovely meeting you and Halfie. I hope you feel better tomorrow."

"Thank you, Lily. That's very kind of you."

Drawing magic, I made my doorway. If times were different, I could see myself being friends with Marian. She seemed like a genuinely kind person, and, of course, she loved squirrels and baked delicious muffins. If our questioning led to her losing her job, I'd feel so guilty, but as she'd said, Mrs Fairchild deserved justice. We'd better get it.

CHAPTER 9

That evening, everyone sat around a massive dining-room table. Angelica had replaced the smaller table in the kitchen/family room with a twelve-seater. Imani had moved in too—just in case. Angelica claimed she wouldn't have to worry so much about her, and it would mean no one would have to do extra protection spells on her house. It also made impromptu meetings, such as this one, easier to organise.

Mum had whipped up a delicious dinner of pork roast with crackling. Ted sat under the table, waiting for scraps. Abby sat on a chair, a small plate in front of her. We hadn't wanted to, but she warned of all the annoying cat stuff she could do to us for the next week. We relented. And didn't she look pleased as punch, sitting up straight, a regal expression on her face.

Angelica dabbed her lips with her napkin, then rested it back on her lap. "I've had time to go through all those documents...." She eyed Millicent and Liv. "Thank you, ladies, for digging up those bank statements and share-trading information."

Millicent smiled. "I wasn't going to let Mr Fairchild off that lightly. I warned him we had the legal right to those documents and the means to obtain them. Now it's a strike against his name if we end up arresting him for the crime."

"Indeed it is." Angelica smiled, which made me smile. She loved getting the better of dishonest people. It was a trait we shared. "According to the documents, the restitution payment to the aggrieved clients was made yesterday." She paused, maybe for dramatic effect, or maybe because she wanted us to voice our own conclusions.

Imani's eyebrows lifted. "That's more than interesting."

"Indeed it is, dear. Could our Mr Fairchild have killed his wife or arranged to kill her to save face and business?"

Will scratched the side of his head. "That sounds like a solid motive to me."

James swallowed his food. "If that's true, how did he get around my talent?"

"Also," said Beren, "motive is not proof. What proof do we have that he cast the spell that killed his wife? This isn't enough to arrest him."

Angelica shifted her gaze to her nephew, who sat next to her. "Yes, dear, I'm well aware. There's a piece missing, and I still want to interview those clients and get an idea of what was said to them about the money and who said it. We have a business address for one and only a PO box for the other." She looked at Will. "I'd like you and Lily to visit the PO box and take photos of who opened it."

"We can do that after dark tonight if you like. There'll be fewer people around."

"Thank you." She looked at James. "I'd like you and Beren

to go to the business address first thing in the morning and see if you can get an interview straight away."

James gave a nod. "Consider it done."

"What about the hairdresser lady? She lied to us too." I didn't want them to forget her. If she was horrible and crazy enough to lie about her client to everyone and risk a defamation suit, she had the potential to do some other crazy stuff, like kill her.

"Her motive isn't as strong, dear, and she's not a witch, but we'll look into her as well. I think we need to start by asking if she'd been to their offices at all." She looked at Imani. "Can you grab a picture of the hairdresser and her daughter and take them to the Fairchilds' offices. Ask the receptionist and Mrs Fairchild's secretary if they've seen her around there."

"Yes, Ma'am."

"And that covers everything I wanted to talk about tonight. I think we should enjoy the rest of our dinner in peace."

"Amen to that," my mother said. I smiled. She'd been so much happier since starting back at the PIB, even in her lessened capacity. Maybe she would be fine without her magic.

After dinner, my stomach felt like it was going to burst. "I may have had one helping too many."

Will's eyes widened. "No! I didn't think that was possible."

"Ha ha, very funny." I looked at Angelica, hopeful she'd say yes to my question. "Is it okay if I go outside and water the garden, commune with the squirrels? I need to walk off my meal and improve my mental health."

"Yes, dear. But keep it to ten minutes, and wear a hat."

"A hat?" It was early evening, and the light was fading. It wasn't like I could get sunburnt.

"Yes. A broad-brimmed one."

"I don't have one."

Her magic tingled my scalp, and one appeared on my head. "Now you do." She smiled.

"But why?" I didn't care if I had to wear one, but curiosity and all that. Also, I probably shouldn't be prodding the bear— she'd said I could go outside. I didn't want her to change her mind because I was being difficult.

"Satellites. Witches use technology, too, dear. And some-times mix it with spells. I wouldn't put it past them to have one that picks out who people are from an aerial shot. The risk, I'll admit, is minimal, but one can never be too careful. If this place is compromised, we're running out of places to live that are set up, ready to go."

"Ah, okay. Thanks for explaining." I rose and placed a hand on my tummy. "Let's get you outside."

Millicent's mouth dropped open. "You're not pregnant, are you?" Everyone's gazes shot to me.

I laughed. "Unless you want to call two servings of pork and roast vegetables a baby, then no, I'm not."

My mother sighed. "It wouldn't be the end of the world, darling. I'd rather like to be a grandmother for the second time."

"Let me enjoy my twenties, and maybe after that I'll consider it." Before they could start planning for me to be pregnant the day after my thirtieth birthday, I jammed the hat on my head and made a break for the back door.

The fresh, balmy air enveloped me as soon as I stepped outside. I shut my eyes and took a long swig through my nose. "Ah, heaven." I stood that way for a moment, just listening to birdsong and crickets. I kind of felt like Snow White. All I needed was a boofy dress and some woodland creatures swarming me.

I opened my eyes and headed for the hose. I turned it on. It unfurled as I walked towards one of the garden beds containing lavender bushes and hedges. Angelica had an automatic watering system, so this wasn't necessary, but it'd been so long since I'd watered a garden, and it was such a relaxing thing to do. The last time I'd done this was probably when I was about fourteen, just after my parents disappeared. It had helped me in moments I felt like I'd been drowning in grief. Just to go outside and realise something bigger than me, than all of us, existed.

I pressed the trigger on the hose attachment, and all I got was a dribble and hissing from further down the hose. I turned and looked back. Argh, stupid kink. Rather than magic it out and risk discovery from any passing witches—there were probably none, but one could never be too careful—I walked back and fixed it with my own two hands.

Next time I pulled the trigger, water gushed out. I adjusted the nozzle to the rain setting and stood in a trance as it flowed over the garden. Hmm, hang on a minute. One of the pictures I'd taken, the one of the room before anything happened, popped into my brain.

The nozzle for the fire sprinkler system. My forehead tightened. Could someone send magic through those pipes?

Peace and quiet forgotten—man, I had a short attention span—I turned off the hose and ran to the back door.

I leaped inside and ran straight to the table. "I think I know!"

Millicent started, Imani raised one brow, and Angelica gave me a deadpan look. "What do you think you know, dear?"

"I think I've worked out how the killer got the lightning to Mrs Fairchild."

Will chuckled. "We should send you to water the garden more often."

"Well, we're waiting." Angelica was about as patient as me sometimes.

"Remember the picture of the boardroom Mrs Fairchild was killed in? Well, right where the lightning started is a sprinkler head. Is it possible that someone sent magic through a different sprinkler head, and it travelled through the pipes and came out at that one?"

Angelica's expression said she was impressed. Yay, me! "I do believe it is possible."

Mum sat forward and looked at her. "That would also explain the paint residue."

Angelica nodded. "Hmm, it would." She looked at James. "Let's set up a test at headquarters. Grab a training dummy, and we'll send a spell from my office to yours." She turned her attention to Will. "While we do that, you and Lily visit that PO box."

I shut and locked the French doors to the green serenity. How silly was I, giving up time out there. But my ideas, when they came, couldn't be ignored. I looked at Will. "Do you have coordinates?"

"Looking them up right now." He typed something into an app on his phone. "Got them. I'll make the doorway. We'll come out in a public toilet about two blocks from our destination."

"Sounds good to me. I need the walk." I patted my rounded tummy.

"Good luck, love." Imani waved.

"Thanks. Hope you guys prove my theory." I put the hat on the table, waved, then stepped through the doorway, covering my mouth and nose with my hand because Will had likely deposited us in a men's toilet. Yep. I hurried out of the door and realised my mistake too late. I should've stopped and listened first. A shocked man standing at the trough jerked his head around. Oh, God. He'd accidentally turned his whole body, and, let's just say, what a mess. "Sorry!"

As I pushed through the main doorway to outside, Will's apologetic voice reached me. "So sorry, mate. You know how it is."

I laughed. What else could I do? I'd never partaken of toilet-cubicle shenanigans. It was a reputation I now had with one person in England. Hopefully I would never see that man again. Will finally made it outside. I swatted his arm.

"Hey, what was that for?"

I rolled my eyes. "What do you think?"

He smirked. "What other excuse could I give? That you were wiping my bottom?"

I snorted. "Yes. That's exactly what you should've said. And ew. I hope I never have to do that."

"I'll try not to get dementia or break both arms while we're together. Okay?"

"Deal." Beren could heal broken arms so that probably wouldn't be an issue, but witches couldn't, as yet, heal dementia. If we managed to fix the PIB situation, maybe we could add a medical research arm? We should really let the wider world know about us. Even if we couldn't, maybe we could partner with human researchers who swore the oath, and they could help marry magic to non-witch methods so that the cure could be administered without suspicion. So what if they took all the credit?

"Lily, we have to go."

"Oh, sorry."

He looked to the heavens, then grabbed my hand. "Just in case you get distracted again, I'll help you get there." His hand was warm and still made my heart and stomach flutter. I smiled. How lucky was I.

"Where are we?"

"Sevenoaks."

"Ah, I thought it looked familiar." The shops were a mix of character buildings and 1970s ugliness. The post office was a large, unfortunate-looking red-brick building that occupied a corner position. We went inside to the section with the post-office boxes. We found the one we wanted, and I stood slightly back from it. I held up my phone. *Show me the person who owns this post-office box.*

I wasn't sure if I was shocked or not. Had I been expecting Mr Fairchild to show up on my screen? Maybe subconsciously? I certainly expected someone from the office, and he was the most likely. Client my bottom. I clicked off a couple of shots, making sure I got him from behind, opening the post-office box, and from the front, walking towards me away from it. No one could argue with that. Although we couldn't use these in court. It might be enough that Angelica could get security footage from the post office that showed him collecting his mail.

Even if he didn't kill his wife, did this mean he was trying to scam his own company?

My head spun with all the thought offshoots that came with that realisation.

"Show me." I handed Will the phone. "Aha! Got him."

"Seems like it. Do you think he was trying to steal company money and she found out, confronted him, and he killed her?"

"That would be the logical answer. We're building a good case against him, but we still have questions that need answering before we arrest him. Let's cross our fingers we have the right person, and we can get the rest of the evidence." Will grabbed my hand. "Let's head back."

As we hurried back to the public toilets, a pang of sadness drifted through me. If my life was normal, I'd be able to wander these streets, do a spot of shopping, stop and have a meal in a café…. I stared at the shopfronts longingly as we rushed past. I clung to the hope that one day this would all be over… the running, hiding, battling, worrying, and we'd still be alive to enjoy what came next. We deserved a happy ending, didn't we?

Unfortunately, people didn't always get what they deserved.

CHAPTER 10

After reaching the country house, we didn't have to wait too long for everyone else to return. Will and I sat in the family room with Mum, Liv, and Millicent. When the others came through the door, their smiles said it all. Angelica stood behind the chair opposite mine and looked down at me. "Nice work, dear. Your theory pans out. Paint residue in the same state as what we found on the body ended up on the dummy. We had to try a few times to get the position of the dummy right, but we were also able to recreate the trajectory from forehead to chest."

James stood behind Millicent's chair and massaged her shoulders. "Now all we have to do is check on that other client tomorrow. What did you lot find out?"

Will looked at me. "You can tell them. You took the photos, after all."

"But you're the agent." It was nice that he wanted me to take the credit, but I'd just as happily not remind Angelica how useful my skill was. Although, that horse had bolted, but you couldn't blame me for trying to stay away from as much PIB work as I could.

Wrinkles appeared on his forehead. "Are you sure? Without you, we wouldn't have gotten that information."

"Oh, for Pete's sake, just tell us!" Imani lifted her hands and slapped the sides of her legs. Her expression was rather aggressive.

I smirked. "You're always sooooo impatient. Such a bad trait." She narrowed her eyes, but I saw her mouth twitch.

"Fine, Lily. I'll tell them." Thank you, Will. "Mr Fairchild owns that PO box."

Angelica pinched her chin between thumb and forefinger. "Interesting. I thought that was an option, but I wouldn't have bet on it. That changes things." She turned to James. "I would imagine the property you're visiting tomorrow will be a friend of his, or maybe a fake address. Maybe you should just do it now."

"Yes, Ma'am." James turned to Beren. "I'll make the doorway." He looked up the address on his phone and then shut his eyes—probably imagining the witchy map of the world that appeared when we needed to see what landing spots were available. Soon enough, he opened his eyes. "Got it." He made the portal, and Beren stepped through first.

While they were gone, Mum served dessert—Portuguese custard tarts. Yum! It was a good distraction until the boys returned. A few minutes later, they came back. Beren entered first. "The address was a small, vacant office. We asked at the kebab shop two doors down, and they said a guy comes by every now and then to collect the mail, and he grabs food from their shop on occasion. We showed him a photo of Mr Fairchild, and bingo."

"Right, well, he's certainly looking good for it. Tomorrow we'll search his office again. We'll need evidence that there's a bit of paint missing from the sprinkler head, and Lily can also take photos, so we know what we're dealing with for sure. We can also take a paint sample to match to the residue."

James sat next to Millicent and growled. "How the hell did he subvert my talent?"

I frowned. His frustration was understandable. Being able to magic was awesome in itself, but having something that you could do better than most others was even more special. To have that questioned or not working properly, well, it was scary. It was like being a top football goal scorer who suddenly lost the ability to score goals, or a world-class sprinter who lost their speed.

Angelica gave him a firm look and used her school-teacher voice. "There will be a good reason. Don't doubt yourself. It's a waste of time at this point. Until we know whether he has his own talent of persuasion or a magical item of some sort, blaming yourself is premature. Am I understood?"

It took a while for his gaze to travel from the table to Angelica's face. "Yes, Ma'am." Millicent grabbed his hand and kissed his cheek. As if they didn't have enough to deal with right now.

"Where's Annabelle?" I'd assumed she would come and live here, but maybe here wasn't safe because of our prisoners. And I guessed Mill and James were busy running in and out and didn't have time over the next few days to look after her properly.

Mill turned sad eyes my way. "My parents are looking after her. They're at their holiday home in Spain. James and Dad put up every protection spell known to man. Their name isn't on the ownership papers, so they shouldn't be able to trace them there. We'll pop over and see her tomorrow morning, early, give her breakfast, then go to work."

It was James's turn to comfort her. He slid his arm around

her shoulder and rubbed her arm. "This'll be over soon. I promise."

Angelica looked at him with an expression that said, "don't make promises you can't keep," but she said, "Time to clean up. We all need a good night's sleep. Tomorrow, we can hopefully close this case and make Phillip happy." She and James shared a look. I narrowed my eyes. What weren't they telling us? I wasn't going to ask because I knew they'd never tell. If they'd stayed silent thus far, they obviously weren't ready to divulge whatever it was.

The light outside was almost gone, and even though it wasn't late, I yawned. Maybe an early night was just what I needed. Maybe a bubble bath first, though. I stood. "I'm going to listen for once and get up to bed. There's a bubble bath with my name on it too."

Angelica smiled. "Yes, the oversized baths in this place are just the thing after a stressful day. Sleep well, dear. You did well today. Thank you."

I smiled. "Any time. Well, not *any* time… just until we get this drama sorted. I still haven't forgotten my dream of being a creative photographer for a living. One of these days."

Mum looked at me, love in her eyes. "Hold onto that thought, darling. It's coming. I can feel it."

I went to her and gave her a hug. "When this is all over, Will and I were thinking a group trip to Australia would be just the thing."

Mum blinked, as if taken off guard. After a moment of consideration, she nodded. "I agree." When we got her back, the first few weeks we hardly ever saw eye to eye, but slowly and surely, our relationship was returning to what it used to be. Even throughout all the turmoil, there was joy. It would have to be enough for today. And it was.

I bade goodnight to everyone else and made my way upstairs. *Bubble bath, here I come.*

The next morning, Angelica, Will, and I dressed in our uniforms, had breakfast, and were ready to go at nine sharp. We wanted to get into Mr Fairchild's office as soon as it opened. If the sprinkler head showed evidence of magic, it would be enough to arrest him. We could confiscate his computers and hopefully confirm that he was the one who owned the two different bank accounts the money was paid into.

What I couldn't work out was why he wanted to rip off his own company. He and Mrs Fairchild were rich and lived a life of extreme luxury. Was Mrs Fairchild tight with the purse strings? Was he trying to get back at her or trying to prove to himself that he could do whatever he wanted, despite what she wanted? We wouldn't know unless he told us. Hopefully he'd be like one of those criminals in the movies who spilt everything when they were caught.

"Can I please come?" At this stage, it was a matter of pride with James. He wanted another crack at the man, I surmised.

"No, dear. I don't want to jeopardise the arrest. If he calls in his lawyer and they know about your talent, they can use that against us. I'd like to figure out why without him being any the wiser."

"It's not like I'd say anything." He gave her his most earnest look.

"No. I need you on the Manners case this morning. And be careful. Our enemies might have some idea of what we're working on. They could be waiting for you if they've worked out who we need to interview. Will almost copped it the other day."

"That was different. They blew my house up to draw us there." The heat in his tone was more than I'd ever heard him use with Angelica. I hoped she took it easy on him—he was hurting on two fronts.

"Yes, but they're waiting for their opportunity. Let's not give it to them. Make sure Beren is with you at all times, please. Look out for each other. You know how that goes."

Beren put a hand on James's shoulder and gently squeezed. "Come on, mate. You know she's right. Let's go do our jobs on this other case. We're so close to cracking it. That dead family deserves just as much justice as Mrs Fairchild, and her case is all but solved."

James took a deep, shuddering breath. He put his hands on his hips and hung his head for a moment. When he raised his head again, all trace of despair was gone. Poker face engaged, he was ready to work. The tension in my shoulders seeped out, and I gave him a sympathetic look. He gave me a chin tip, and he and Beren made doorways to headquarters.

Angelica made a doorway. "Okay, you two. Let's go."

I brought my Nikon again. Professional as always. Angelica buzzed their reception-room door, and the automatic opening mechanism clicked soon after. The receptionist could see us on a video feed. As we reached the desk, she was hanging the phone up. She eyed off Will first and gave him a bright smile. He didn't return it.

"Good morning, Anthea. We'd like to see Mr Fairchild if he's in." Good old Angelica, straight to the point.

"I'm afraid he's not in yet." Her gaze strayed to the floor before meeting Angelica's again. "Would you like me to tell him you've been?" If that wasn't a fob off, I didn't know what was. If only James was here to let us know if she was lying, although, I'm sure Angelica had a good idea with most people. Body language was still a cue, and she'd given us one with that eye dip.

"That's fine." She turned to Will as if dismissing the woman. "Can I have the search warrant, please?"

He smiled. "Yes, Ma'am." His magic tickled my scalp, and a piece of paper appeared in his hand. He gave it to her.

Angelica passed it to Anthea. "We'll try not to make too much of a mess." She watched as the woman read the warrant. When the receptionist was done, she reached for the phone on her desk. "I'm afraid not. We can't have you interfering with an investigation."

Anthea stared defiantly at Angelica and took the receiver off its cradle.

Angelica drew magic, and the woman froze. "Think yourself lucky that I'm not arresting you for hindering an investigation." I could only guess at what the receptionist thought about that because her features were frozen in that "I'll show you" expression. Ah, the irony. I chuckled, because who wouldn't, and Angelica gave me a reproving look. "It's not nice to gloat, dear."

"But I'm only human."

Angelica's lip twitched up at that. She snatched the warrant out of Anthea's rigid fingers. "Come on. Let's get this done."

We went through the door to the offices, and the receptionist couldn't even turn her head to watch us. That kept me smiling for a while longer.

The walk to Mr Fairchild's office took a couple of minutes. This place was huge. His door was shut, and Angelica knocked.

"Come in."

Boy, was he going to be surprised.

I made sure my return to sender was up. Not that I thought he'd attack me, but it would be stupid of me not to be cautious. Will opened the door and motioned for Angelica to enter first. Such a gentleman. He also waited for me to go in before he entered and shut the door.

Mr Fairchild sat in a luxurious rich-brown leather chair at a mahogany desk. Shelves behind him on the wall contained pictures of him at numerous black-tie events with famous people. I recognised a few of them—actors and musicians. This guy was all about the image, apparently. There was also a picture of him sitting in a red Ferrari and one of him at the helm of what appeared to be an expensive luxury motorboat. His eyebrows almost reached his hairline. "Wh— I... I said I wasn't to be disturbed." His expression recovered, settling into mild anger. He stood. "I'll have to have a word with my receptionist, not warning me. What's the meaning of you just barging in here?"

Her expression mild, Angelica handed him a piece of paper. "That's a search warrant. You're free to observe or not, but you can't leave these offices." His eyes widened, and he sucked in a lungful of air, no doubt to put power into the outrage he wanted to spew. Angelica cut him off with her hand held aloft. "I don't want to hear it. This is an ongoing investigation. Do you want us to find out what happened to your beloved wife or not?" I loved it when she asked provocative questions.

Mr Fairchild's face twisted with the injustice of it all. To answer or not to answer honestly, that was the question. Maybe hoping he was still going to escape detection, he sputtered, "Fine. Of course. But I don't see how you're going to find anything in my office that will tie me to her death." His face calmed, and the aggro leeched from his eyes. "I loved my wife. I didn't kill her."

"Well then, you have nothing to worry about, do you?" Angelica's poker face was back. She'd stopped playing. Now it was time to get down to business. She turned to Will. "Please make sure he doesn't go anywhere."

He gave a nod. "Yes, Ma'am."

If looks could kill, Will would be on the floor breathing his last breath. Shame Mr Fairchild didn't like Will as much as the receptionist did.

Mr Fairchild sat again and stared at Angelica. It would be more difficult for me to take my pictures, but it was still doable because I had an excuse to photograph the area around the sprinkler head. It would take a second for me to ascertain whether or not he'd cast the spell from here. If not, I didn't know what Angelica wanted to do next. Maybe visit every office and see who'd done it.

She looked at me. "Agent Bianchi, please get to work. We haven't got all day." I knew what she was asking. Her no-nonsense tone was for Mr Fairchild's benefit, so was the continuation of my agent name.

"Yes, Ma'am." My stomach flipped as nervousness took hold. I didn't have an emotional attachment to the victim, but there was excitement in solving crimes. It would be disappointing if my theory didn't pan out. I found that I really, really wanted the evidence to show up in my camera.

I drew magic and turned my camera on, pointing it at the sprinkler head. *Show me Mr Fairchild casting the spell that killed Mrs Fairchild.* There he was, standing in front of his desk, arms lifted, hands splayed towards the sprinkler. Concentration poured from his face. The blue glow of magic surrounded him.

Bingo! *Click.*

I looked at Angelica and gave her the slightest of nods. She wanted to inspect the sprinkler head, but that might be too obvious, so she turned to Mr Fairchild, who sent a scathing gaze her way. "Mr Fairchild, this warrant entitles us to look at your computers, any paperwork here or at your home, or at any other places of work you may have."

He sputtered, shooting to his feet. His magic prickled my scalp. "Y-you can't!"

Her tone brooked no argument. "I can. And I will." She gave Will a look.

He cast a freeze spell on Mr Fairchild. "We're putting you under a freeze spell for threatening an agent. Drawing magic is seen as intent to do harm or tamper with evidence." Hadn't heard that one before, but it made total sense. Angelica was now free to look around. She and Will tore through the office. Using magic, they mined every piece of paper they needed. They magicked away his laptop and desktop.

Will magicked a ladder from who knew where, and Angelica climbed it, magnifying glass in hand. As she examined the sprinkler head, I looked at Fairchild in disappointment. What a shame Will had frozen him. It would've been satisfying to see his panicked expression. A small scraping tool and plastic bag appeared, floating next to the ceiling. The tool then scraped paint from the sprinkler head into the bag. The bag sealed itself, then disappeared, likely off to Floyd.

Will's phone rang. "Agent Blakesley speaking." He cocked his head to one side as he listened. "Great. Please email it now. Thanks. Bye."

Angelica descended the ladder. "Who was that?"

"Olivia with some bank statements."

She nodded and allowed a small smile to grace her face. "We'll take a quick look; then you can arrest our suspect." She waved her arm, and the ladder disappeared. I always loved a bit of theatrics when casting spells. Why waste the opportunity?

Will opened his phone and brought up the documents, skimming through them one at a time. It took a few minutes. When he was done, he handed the phone to Angelica. After another few minutes, she gave the phone back and took handcuffs from her pocket. Usually, she left the arresting to others, but maybe this was slightly personal, since a friend of hers asked her specifically to solve this one.

"Marcus Fairchild, you're under arrest for the murder of Adelaide Fairchild." She slipped the cuffs on him, and Will dropped the freeze spell. Satisfaction spread through my chest, warm and joyful.

Will made a doorway to the PIB reception room.

"I didn't do it! You can't arrest me!"

"We're going to do this, are we?" Angelica raised a brow. "I'm not going to give away all our secrets, but we know your aliases. We know you faked documents showing you bought shares for those two aliases and sold them for a massive loss. We also know you then defrauded your own company of the money by having that money 'paid back' to those 'clients.'"

His nervous laughter was telling. "You can't prove anything. Also, how is it a crime to take money from your own company?"

"It's fraud and theft when that company is either partly or mostly owned by your wife. She let you put your name on the door, but it was funded by her money, and she owned 80 per cent of it, did she not?"

"How did you know?" Wow, this guy was the king of stupid questions.

Angelica rolled her eyes. "Let's get him out of here."

Will grabbed his arm and was about to pull him through.

A thought popped into my head. "As much as that floozy at the front desk annoys me with her cow eyes at you, Agent

Blakesley, shouldn't someone unfreeze her? She's going to have to go to the toilet at some point."

"Oh, right you are, dear." Angelica waved her hand again, and I could only assume the woman had her faculties back. "You can go back to you know where while we take him in. We'll see you later."

"Okay, bye." They disappeared through the doorway and left me by myself. I wandered to his shelves to more closely inspect his photos. Greed got to this guy. Or maybe it was a fragile ego—his wife was the more successful one, and he operated under her say so. It would be a long time before he got to drive his classic Ferrari or hobnob with the rich and famous. Idiot. Well, he only had himself to blame.

Another crime solved. I grinned. We did good. The only problem was that the business would likely have to shut down. Marian would lose her job. That made me momentarily sad, but from what she said and from what I'd seen, she'd find another good job. Hopefully even better than this one. I decided to give her a heads-up, so she could start looking immediately.

As I created my doorway, I dialled Marian's number. If only all my decisions could be so easy.

CHAPTER 11

Everyone had gotten home late that night, so Mum, Liv, and I ate dinner by ourselves. I was fast asleep when Will came home. Thankfully, he was next to me when I awoke just after eight thirty. "How did you go last night?" I asked, yawning.

"He got a solicitor, but once we started laying out our proof, he caved and admitted his guilt."

"Wow, that didn't take long."

"We gave him a plea deal. Angelica okayed it with Mrs Fairchild's second cousin. Now we can get back to those other cases. Oh, we also found out from his mother that his talent is lying."

"Whoa! That'll make James feel better. He'll probably still be a bit cut up about it, but at least he'll know he's not losing his magical mojo."

"Yep. Angelica told him as soon as we found out."

I ran a hand down his cheek. "What about the directors and the prices on our heads? We need to deal with it. Maybe once they're gone, we can get the PIB back to its former glory."

Worry hazed his grey eyes. "We'll be talking about it today. Breakfast meeting at nine. What time is it?"

I turned around and checked my alarm clock. Eight thirty-seven. Suppose we should get up."

We washed our faces, brushed our teeth, and dressed. By the time we made it down to the family room, everyone else was there, seated around the table. Plates were set, and an array of food sat in a line along the middle of the table. Lots of people meant lots of food.

My gaze snagged on a stranger sitting next to Angelica. He was an older, distinguished gentleman, probably in his sixties, his soft grey hair cut neatly but not shaved. He wore a yellow polo shirt and a friendly smile.

Angelica put a hand on his forearm. "This is Phillip, Mrs Fairchild's second cousin and a close friend of mine. This is Lily and William."

I suppressed my surprise. He was supposed to be an acquaintance, but now he was a close friend? Was that because she'd solved the crime, or had she wanted to keep their closeness under wraps for some reason?

Will jumped in while I recovered. He approached the man and offered his hand to shake. "Lovely to meet you, Phillip."

"Ah, hi. I'm Lily."

"Pleased to meet you both. I've heard so much about you from Angie."

I blinked. Angie? How was he still alive right now? The way he looked at Angelica was… affectionate, familiar. What in the squirrel's nest? Was it too early for alcohol?

Will and I sat in our places. Thankfully, I was also next to Imani. She could talk me down or at least make me laugh. She leaned over and whispered, "You look a little… shellshocked, love."

"Um… you could say that. How's your day going?"

She chuckled. "Surprisingly, but not terribly. Look, we have French toast!"

Indeed we did. Scrumptious food could soften any blow… well, almost any. I tucked right in. And look, it wasn't that I didn't want Angelica to have romantic love; it was just… such a surprise. And who was this guy? I mean, I knew his name and that he was rich and powerful, but was he nice? Was he deserving of one of the strongest, bravest women I knew? Why had she kept it a secret, or was it a recent thing? So many questions, none of which would likely be answered this morning.

"Right, now that we're all here, we have a few things to discuss." Her voice was businesslike, but a chill ran down my back. Premonitions weren't my talent. There was probably a quality to her tone that my subconscious recognised. Everyone else must've recognised it, too, because we all stopped whatever we were doing and stared at her. "As you know, Phillip is Mrs Fairchild's second cousin. He also holds a lot of sway with existing members of parliament and the royal family." She turned and gave him a gentle look. "I'll let you explain the rest."

The smile he gave her brimmed with affection and gratitude. "Thank you, my love." Well, that progressed quickly. We were only just meeting her new boyfriend, and all of a sudden, they're already in love? How new was this relationship? It kind of hurt that she was this serious about someone but had kept it from us for goodness knew how long. Although, my mother didn't look as shocked as the rest of us… neither did my brother. Hmm….

He placed his hands in his lap and looked around the table

at each of us in turn. His manner was relaxed. Such a chilled vibe. They did say opposites attracted. Angelica usually maintained an outward appearance of calm, but it was laced with the sense that she could get angry at any moment and scold you. He had none of that. If my radar was right, he was actually a nice person. "I know my relationship with Angie has taken most of you by surprise. I want to assure you that I'm extremely fond of her, and I will never do anything to hurt her." His expression saddened. "I also want to thank you for getting to the bottom of my cousin's murder. I understand I called in a special favour. Please know that it's deeply appreciated. When Angie agreed to push aside other investigations, it came to my attention why she was reluctant to." He gave her a look that said "you should have come to me sooner."

She pressed her lips together. "I don't like asking for help. And this is political—you could end up with more enemies. I promised I would never involve you in my problems, yet here we are." I shared a confused look with Will. She was spilling secrets faster than a three-year-old spilt red cordial whilst running across white carpet.

Phillip watched her as he answered, "I assure you that I don't care about that. I've had many enemies for many years, yet it hasn't affected my life one iota." He looked to the rest of us again. "I hear you have a problem with the PIB board of directors and their... *associates*."

I swallowed. We were going to go there?

I flicked my gaze to Angelica. She'd donned her poker face. My belly gurgled as a tumbleweed of trepidation blew through it. She must have thought we couldn't win this thing by ourselves any more. I didn't know if Will could sense my fear, but he grabbed my hand and squeezed. Angelica asking for help was akin to her giving up.

Were we all goners?

But surely she wouldn't involve someone else she loved if things were hopeless. I held onto that thought as tightly as I held Will's hand.

Phillip opened his mouth to speak again, and Angelica's steadfast gaze moved to me… and stayed. I swallowed. Something bad was coming. I just knew it. The need to run back to the old home and sit amongst my squirrel army overcame me. My heart ached for simpler days, days that were beyond my reach and might be forevermore.

Even though Phillip had a kind visage, when he looked at me, all I could see was a threat. What was he going to ask in return for helping us? "Lily, I hear you have many special talents." It was as if ice water had been poured over my head. Shivers vibrated down my nape and shoulders. Will squeezed my hand tighter. I glanced at him. His jaw was bunched, his forehead deeply creased.

I stared at Angelica. Regret hijacked her steadfast expression. That was likely the only apology I was getting.

Thoughts shot around my brain, but which one to go with first? I hated the feeling of vulnerability, like I was sitting here naked. It would be easy to lose my grasp on good sense and ask why she'd done this. But our lives obviously depended on it; otherwise, there was no way she'd divulge my secrets. I shut my eyes and took a deep breath, slowing my thoughts. I opened my eyes again. "Yes." That was all I could manage.

"We're interested in one particular one."

"*We?*"

"MI6."

Will tensed. "The spy agency?"

He met Will's question with a serene stare, as if a deal had already been negotiated. "Yes. We've agreed to lend our expertise and resources to your current… situation. In return, we require your assistance on an extremely delicate internal matter." He looked at me. "In particular, we require this young lady's assistance."

Imani rubbed my back. "It's okay, love. Whatever you decide, we're with you."

I tamped down the fear urging me to say no. "How many people would find out my secret?"

"Three others. The head of MI6 and two of their best operatives."

"Are they witches?" Not that it mattered, but the more information I had, the better.

"Only one of the operatives is. We have an agreement, as per the Queen's directive. She doesn't want too many witches in places of power in our government departments or forces. If any go rogue, they can do more damage than a non-witch. The status quo needs to be retained. I can assure you that all three will be made to swear to silence on your talent. No one else will find out."

Holy moly. This was getting complicated. As much as witches helped humans, of course they were scared of us. There was no way we could ever go public with who we were. It would start a war. Fear was the beginning of so many bad situations. "How long would you need me for?"

He smoothed his eyebrows, one at a time, with two fingers. "Maybe a week or two, but if that works out, we would likely require your services on occasion."

I shot Angelica an irritated glare. "Would I be indebted for life?"

"No, dear. Our deal is for one year."

"Do I have time to consider this?"

She shook her head. "They need to know so they can plan their next move. If we agree to this, I'll be with you every step of the way. As well as helping us, we'd become a special branch of MI6. We'd keep the agency name and run it ourselves, but we'd be funded directly by MI6. The PIB would survive, and you know how important that is."

I blew out a huge breath. "Yes, I do." I looked at Phillip. "How are you going to help us with our current *situation*?"

"We have information on the cartels involved with the directors. We can also offer manpower, elite soldiers who know about witches and are trained in combat against them. We believe if planned right, we can take them all down in one night, and you'll all be free to do your jobs as you used to. Angie will take with her those agents she implicitly trusts, and we'll help her hire and train other trustworthy witches and non-witches. I have instructions to integrate more non-witches into important positions within the PIB. They will report directly to me, and thus, the Queen's people."

Angelica smoothed her ever-present bun. "If you agree to this, we can continue to make a positive difference. We have a greater chance of overcoming the directors and getting on with our lives."

I scrubbed my face. Would my life be in any more danger than it already was? Not really. The spies they told were being made to swear on a spell, and provided we managed to get rid of the directors, I'd be safer. Sacrificing another year of my life was a small price to pay for this deal. Hopefully, Angelica hadn't misplaced her trust. The deal would, however, make it much harder for me to disappear and lead a normal life if MI6 decided they wanted me as a permanent asset. I placed a hand on my stomach in a hopeless effort to settle the churning.

Everyone was staring at me, but I didn't look at them. This had to be my decision. It came down to logic—Angelica felt our situation was worse than dire. I trusted her judgement. If this was the route she thought best, then who was I to argue?

It felt as if I were trying to escape from quicksand—the harder I fought for freedom, the deeper I sank.

Resignation embedded into my heart. As hopes of playing with my beloved squirrels again and seeing our lives return to a semblance of normal blossomed, I met Phillip's stare with a confident one of my own. "I'll do it. I'll help MI6. But I have one condition."

It was as if a valve had been opened, and some of the tension dissipated. I looked at Mum. Her expression was better than I'd thought it would be. A tinge of fear, likely for me, but relief. It surprised me that she agreed with my decision. What had Angelica told her that I wasn't privy to? Whatever it was, it seemed she thought I'd made the right decision. And no one seemed concerned as to what my condition was. It was probably because I was such a pushover where protecting my family was concerned.

Phillip's relieved smile was wide. "Thank you, Lily. You won't regret it. So, what is your condition?"

"Once we've neutralised the directors and their cronies, we get two weeks for a trip to Australia with everyone at this table." I held my breath, hoping he wouldn't shoot it down. If he said no, I wouldn't pull out of the deal, because we needed his help, unfortunately. But he didn't know that, so I crossed my fingers under the table.

He turned to Angelica, and she gave an almost-imperceptible nod. Phillip looked back at me. "I think that can be arranged. You have a deal."

"Thank you."

His tone was serene, as if we were discussing whether his favourite ice cream flavour was vanilla or chocolate. "We'll meet with operatives tomorrow and start planning our assault on your enemies." He peered around the table. "All your lives will be back to normal in no time. I promise."

"In that case, let's eat breakfast." Angelica gave us a genuine, albeit small, smile.

Will turned to me and leaned closer, his soft voice full of reverence. "You're one in a billion, Lily. I'm proud of you. You've given us the best chance to get through this and save the PIB. Thank you." He kissed my cheek.

My cheek tingled, and syrupy warmth trickled over my heart. No matter what happened, Will loved me, and so did my family and friends. Maybe this wasn't going to be as bad as I feared. We now had the support of one of Britain's most powerful institutions.

Chatter slowly ramped up as everyone settled into our new reality. If we survived this, the PIB would live on. Angelica wouldn't have to worry about funding or traitors undermining her. England would be safe from rogue witches.

"Here, love." Imani dropped two pieces of French toast into my plate.

I smiled at her. "Thanks."

As I gazed around the table at my increasingly relaxed and even happy family, I knew I'd made the right decision. Angelica's friend had thrown us a lifeline.

Now we just had to make the most of it.

⊗

The next instalment, *Witch Showdown in Westerham*, will be available November 2022.

If you've enjoyed this book, you might enjoy my new cosy mystery series, Haunting Avery Winters. Book 1—A Killer Welcome.

Avery Winters was overjoyed to be brought back to life… unfortunately, the dead were waiting for her.

Aussie journalist Avery Winters was content—she had a caring boyfriend, great job, and supportive… okay, so her parents weren't actually supportive, but she'd accepted she could never be the son they'd wanted seeing as how she was born a girl. Avoiding them seemed to work well, and, she reasoned, no one's life was perfect.

And that was fine, except whilst covering a news story in a storm, Avery's cosy life disappeared in a flash. Lightning struck, stopping her heart and blowing her favourite black boots to smithereens. It was pure luck that an off-duty nurse was walking nearby.

When Avery came to in the ambulance en route to hospital, she'd thought the worst was over. She was wrong.

Her lightning-induced hallucinations—there was no way they were ghosts—were impossible to hide. Her boyfriend soon left, and her boss suggested she take extended leave. Unable to cover her rent, she moved back in with her parents. And that's when the fun really began. Unable to cope with their insistence she was crazy, and desperate for an escape, she responded to a journalist-wanted ad… in the UK, because getting mega far away from her parents could only be a good thing.

Armed with a new fear of storms, companions others couldn't see, and the hope that leaving the stress behind would improve her mental state, she boarded a plane for London. What she didn't count on was not being able to leave her ghosts behind… literally. Oh, and that the quaint English village she'd be living in had more skeletons in its closet than the Natural History Museum.

When she stumbles upon a dead body in her rented apartment on her first day, she's tempted to get back on the plane. But whilst it's not a good omen, returning to her parents would be worse, so she decides to stay. Only, she's not sure if it's the best decision she's ever made, or the worst.

She's about to find out.

ABOUT THE AUTHOR

USA Today bestselling author, Dionne Lister is a Sydneysider with a degree in creative writing and two Siamese cats. Daydreaming has always been her passion, so writing was a natural progression from staring out the window in primary school, and being an author was a dream she held since childhood.

Unfortunately, writing was only a hobby while Dionne worked as a property valuer in Sydney, until her mid-thirties when she returned to study and completed her creative writing degree. Since then, she has indulged her passion for writing while raising two children with her husband. Her books have attracted praise from Apple iBooks and have reached #1 on Amazon and iBooks charts worldwide, frequently occupying top 100 lists in fantasy and mystery.